VANISHED

An ALIAS, Enemies to Lovers Romantic Suspense

LISA HUGHEY

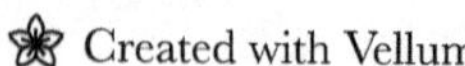 Created with Vellum

To my husband for being my true north and giving his unconditional support. Writing is a tough business (lately even tougher), but he's never suggested that I go get a "real" job so that I could consistently contribute to our family bottom line. Love you!!

Chapter 1

E*dinburgh, Scotland*
"What now, Officer Ballard?" Fiona Thomas, Hamish Ballard's boss at the National Crime Agency, let out a long-suffering sigh.

"I was able to trace Brianna Walsh to America." Hamish leaned forward, perched on the edge of the uncomfortable chair across from his supervisor, as if he could will her to get excited about his success. He had exhausted all his leads on the woman responsible for his brother's death. Until today. Finally, one of his connections at MI5 had managed to give him highly classified information about Brianna. Her last known contact was at some public relations firm, Adams-Larsen Inc. and Associates, in Washington, DC. "She's using the name Beatrice Winter. I want to go—"

"You've got to let go of this obsession." She put her head in her hands.

Brianna Walsh needed to pay. And she needed to be stopped before more people died. "But—"

"No more. If you keep pursuing information about Brianna Walsh, your job is in jeopardy."

He kept his mouth shut but his expression must have given him away. Family was everything. He'd been raised to stick together. He'd forgotten that lesson for a while. But he would never forget again. Blood, family was everything—even in death, blood prevailed.

"Do you understand?" she pressed.

He didn't answer.

Couldn't answer. The rage and frustration that had fueled him for the past year had only grown after it seemed as if Brianna had just…vanished.

"Officer Ballard?"

"Aye, ma'am." Hamish Ballard stood in front of his boss's desk like a little kid in front of the headmaster and nodded while he lied through his teeth.

"Go on holiday for a week and get your head on straight. When you come back, I don't want to hear anything else about the Walsh family. Her father and brothers are in prison. The rest of their empire is in disarray. The Walsh cousins are impotent and ineffective without them. Brianna served the Crown with her testimony. Leave. Off. Full stop."

Hamish had no intention of dropping his quest for justice. He hadn't been there for his brother in life, he wasn't about to abandon him in death. "Aye, ma'am."

"Get on with your fuckin' life, Ham."

He left the office…and headed to the airport.

He'd find his answers in America. In Washington, DC. At a public relations firm of all things.

He had one week to find Brianna Walsh. No fucking way was he letting this—her—go.

SOME DAYS HER MOTTO, No Regrets, was easier to follow than others.

Jillian Larsen, cofounder of Adams-Larsen Inc. and Associates, affectionately nicknamed ALIAS, headed down the stairs of the office brownstone to grab a cup of coffee from the credenza in the former dining room that now served as her company's conference room.

The office was buzzing after the long holiday weekend. Everyone was chatting about what they had done over Thanksgiving. Jill had spent the weekend, and the holiday, alone in her rowhouse. Thanksgiving dinner had been leftover takeout, out of the to-go container, at the island bar in her kitchen.

She would never regret what she'd done before starting ALIAS, but sometimes her life was lonely.

"Man, it's good to be home." Jake Brown—in Texas for the past month working with a corporate whistleblower whose company had been dumping toxic waste and falsifying data reports to the state government—had missed her increasingly vague deflections regarding Marsh.

"Welcome back."

"Where is Marsh?" Jake asked as he stirred his coffee with one of the silver spoons.

Jill bit into a sugar cookie in the shape of a rosy-cheeked Santa and sighed. Maria Torres, former receptionist and current field trainee, had been working on her royal icing recipe and if she kept bringing her baked goods to the office, Jill was going to go up a dress size.

And that was a total lie. In reality, she'd lost weight.

Marsh, her absent (and missing) partner, the Adams in

Adams-Larsen, was AWOL. His absence was starting to take a toll. Everyone was pulling extra duty to cover for him. Jill was the face of the company and the person who dealt with their clients. She had the temperament to keep things a secret and to deny potential clients.

Marsh was too nice, always wanting to rescue people. He was their logistics guy, and his three-month unexpected sabbatical had begun to impact their business. If Marsh didn't come back soon, she was going to have to figure something else out.

They kept the business compartmentalized so that if an employee was ever compromised, it would be impossible for them to reveal the specifics of a client relocation. But it also meant that Jill didn't typically dig down into the nitty gritty of relos beyond vetting the potential candidates.

Jill tightened her jaw and forced a smile. "Should be back soon," she said cheerfully.

Jake grinned at her and snatched two cookies off the plate. He lifted them like he was toasting to good news and then sauntered away.

"When *is* Marsh coming back?" Viktor Kuznets tilted his head to the side in question. His eyebrows crimped, his usually perfect arch a bit scraggly and unlike her fastidious friend. She needed to pay more attention to her own house and quit looking for her errant partner.

Viktor had recently broken up with his live-in boyfriend and his attempt to mask his sadness was pretty much a failure, but he didn't let it interfere with his work as their onsite medic, weapons keeper, and skip tracer. Hopefully they wouldn't need his medic services in the near future.

Marsh was the one everyone went to for advice. Their confidant. Viktor clearly needed to talk, and their father figure was nowhere to be found.

"I'll let you know when I have an exact date." Not exactly a lie. "I've got some admin stuff to take care of before the new receptionist gets here. You guys have a good day."

She marched up the stairs of the old brownstone that had been converted into office space and turned at the top to address her employees, who were still watching her. "I'll be in my office if anyone needs me."

Jillian had basically just…Lied. To. Her. Staff.

Her staff was more like her family than her actual family. But there were things they didn't know, things no one knew, except Marsh. And the weight of what she carried was somehow too much these days.

Her carefully constructed world was falling apart.

She'd always thought of herself as confident and secure, sending a giant Fuck You to anyone who judged her, because at the end of the day she knew her core morals were rock solid.

Except she hadn't realized how alone she was until her support system disappeared.

Kita Kim, resident hacker, social media seeder, and their self-defense instructor, followed Jill up the stairs. "Can I talk to you?"

"Always," Jill replied smoothly, her stomach cramping.

"Privately." Kita was the only other employee who knew Marsh was missing. She had also been Marsh's friend since high school.

"Come on in my office."

Once her office door was closed, Kita threw herself into a wing chair. "How are you really?"

Since she'd gotten a boyfriend, Kita had decided to start sharing her feelings. There was a reason that both she and Kita were Marsh's besties. Neither one of them was what you'd call warm and fuzzy. Except lately, the formerly tight-lipped Kita wanted to share. Blech.

"Fine."

Kita rolled her eyes. "Sure. Have you heard from Marsh?"

No. She'd been hoping he'd come home for Thanksgiving and she could rip him a new one and everything would go back to normal.

But that hadn't happened.

And she was at a loss as to what to do next. She wasn't an indecisive person. Far from it. She assessed the situation and then acted based on a set of criteria to fix it. Normally she had an unshakeable sense of purpose.

But things hadn't been normal in a while and at this moment she was floundering. "No."

"What are we going to do?"

Jill had searched everywhere. She'd exhausted all her resources without delving into Marsh's privacy to try to figure out where he had gone. But he'd been off grid for over ten weeks. "Wait until he comes home."

"Wait?" Kita's voice rose.

She hadn't really solidified what her next course of action was until this moment, but she realized now that she was done.

"Yes." Jill nodded. She was done looking for her missing partner. The business needed her attention. Her *life* needed her attention.

Her intercom buzzed. Maria was manning the phones and door waiting for the new receptionist, Hannah Smith, to get here. Hannah had almost become a client a few weeks ago, but Kita had saved her.

Finding employees they trusted was the biggest challenge

at ALIAS. Typically they vetted new employees six ways to Sunday, and potential new hires had a personal recommendation from multiple employees.

Their business was highly secretive. After a career-destroying situation had left her job and reputation at the US Marshals in shambles, she and Marsh had left and formed ALIAS to help relocate people who were not covered by government witness protection programs.

"There's a Hamish Ballard at the front door. He says he needs to see you."

She didn't have a Hamish Ballard on her calendar. "Regarding?"

"He won't say."

Jill punched up the security feed on her desktop computer.

She couldn't see much. Guy in a navy suit. European cut. Dark hair. Broad shoulders. Brawny body, not all that tall. He had his back to the camera as he surveyed their quiet street.

Jill pressed the intercom button. "What can I do for you, Mr. Ballard?"

He turned around. Dark hair brushed away from his face revealed sharp features: raw-boned cheeks, a wide unsmiling mouth, and an assessing gaze. There was a stillness to his stance, an economical way that he moved that made her think law enforcement.

He reached inside his suit coat.

Jill tensed, though she knew that even if he had a weapon, he wasn't breaching the building unless she let him. Their security was top-notch.

He pulled out a leather wallet and flipped it open. "It's Officer Ballard." His accent, a hint of Scottish brogue, sent a shiver through her. Swoony. "I'd like fifteen minutes of your time to discuss a case with you."

"One moment." Jill raised her eyebrows. "Maria, let Officer Ballard in."

Kita grinned. "I'll leave you to the Scottish Hottie. We can chat again later." And she strode from Jill's office.

Well, Hamish Ballard had been good for one thing. She'd gotten rid of Kita without much nudging.

Jill couldn't help the anticipation that cascaded through her. Hopefully Hamish Ballard would take her focus away from her missing partner. The distraction was welcome.

Within a few minutes, Maria ushered the man in to her office.

His presence filled the slightly feminine space as if he had expanded into all the nooks and crannies and sucked out every bit of air. Her body tingled and her heart jolted at the electricity in the room.

Jill met him near the furniture grouping of a small settee and chairs. Up close he was even more attractive than on the video screen. Jill extended her hand for the obligatory business greeting.

The moment their palms touched, an unshakeable sense of connection arced through her. Her gaze met his, a flash of attraction there and then gone.

Jill smoothed her expression and gestured toward a wing chair. "Have a seat." She would admit to being curious. "How can I help you?"

Hopefully he'd have a new project for her to work on. Something to take her mind off Marsh.

He pulled a photograph from the breast pocket of his suit and placed it on the coffee table. "I'm looking for this woman."

"We don't *find* people. We're a public relations firm." But she tilted her head and picked up the photo.

Beatrice Winter. Jill kept her face casually interested but inside her curiosity roused. Adams-Larsen didn't ever give out information on their clients. Ever. People weren't even supposed to know they were connected to their clients.

Jill pretended to study the picture. Beatrice had been an interesting case. A whistleblower for a string of drug rehab centers whose CEO and CFO had pocketed their drug-addicted patients' money, scammed insurance companies for millions, and didn't actually do any rehab treatment. Their relapse rate was almost eighty percent—well above the typical forty to sixty percent. The executives had plead guilty and were awaiting sentencing.

"I'm sorry. I don't know her."

He bristled. "Bollocks."

"Excuse me?" Jill frosted her voice.

"You're lying."

She was. But no way did he know that. More intimidating agents than Officer Hamish Ballard with the charming accent had tried to crack her. Yet his accusation rankled.

Protecting her clients was her number one priority. And she didn't have to take his attitude. "I believe this meeting is done."

He leaned forward in the chair, his eyes intense, harsh. "Not until you tell me where she is or I'll make life very difficult for you. She's a criminal."

His threat was empty and unachievable. Instead of upsetting her, his blustery manner caused her to relax. No way was Beatrice Winter a criminal, but points for creativity.

Pity. Hamish Ballard was a blowhard. She had seen his

type before. All blow, no hard. The dig made her laugh inside, and a little smile curved her mouth at her own private joke.

"This amuses you?" The harsh planes of his face were set in anger, but they were also compellingly attractive. The close-shaved beard and the slightly heavier mustache emphasized lips that looked soft in direct contrast to his hard navy-blue eyes.

And fuck her, he might be a blowhard, but apparently her hormones didn't care.

Well, too damn bad. She was a high-functioning adult, and just because her body was saying *jump him* didn't mean she had to listen.

"Not at all, Mr. Ballard," Jillian said smoothly. "But I don't believe we have anything to discuss."

"*Officer* Ballard," he ground out.

Yes, he'd made that patently clear.

She wondered if he was going to flip open his wallet to show her his shield again.

"I need to know where she is," he demanded once more.

And that tickle of amusement was gone. Her hormones would have to take a flying leap. She wasn't about to get up close and personal with this guy.

Taking her time, Jill circled around her desk, retreating to put a solid object between herself and the increasingly enraged officer.

"First of all, I don't know her or where she is." Jill ticked the items off on her fingers. She didn't raise her voice, but he couldn't miss the obvious: she was pissed. "Secondly, I don't appreciate you coming into my office and insulting me."

"I don't have time for your evasions," he snapped out. "She is wanted in the UK."

Impossible.

Adams-Larsen had relocated her after a *thorough* background check. She'd been vetted from here to Christmas. And the original request for relocation had come directly from Jill's old boss.

She was done totally with him.

He stalked to her desk and slapped the picture on the mahogany surface. "Look again. Her given name is Brianna Walsh."

Nope. Not her name.

"But she was using the alias Beatrice Winter."

Jill's heart rate picked up. But there was no way this woman was wanted. *No way*. Their background investigation process was flawless. She'd been referred to them by the United States Marshals, for fuck's sake. "I don't have any information for you."

His attractive face reddened. "Don't you even want to know what she's guilty of?" His fingers tightened into a fist.

"I'm a very busy woman, Officer Ballard." And he was wasting her time. She waved her hand toward the door and pretty much indicated that he get out.

He took an audible breath and visibly reined in his temper. "You need to listen to me."

She really didn't.

"I know that Adams-Larsen had something to do with the disappearance of Beatrice Winter."

He was right, but no way would she admit a thing. Even if he pressed her harder.

"What I don't understand is why you'd be hiding a supposed whistleblower in the first place."

"Because I'm not." And technically Beatrice wasn't hidden. Just relocated with a new name and a new job and a new life.

Because the Marshals had a leak in their office, so her old boss, Deanna Womack, had asked for a favor. And she and Marsh had agreed.

On the surface, the Marshals office had fired Jill over an ethics breach. But the truth was a lot more complicated. A pang of sadness hit her.

With Marsh gone, it really underscored her lonely life. She'd given up a lot more than her career with the Marshals when her lover, Dominic, had officially died under her protection.

But that was ancient history and she made it her personal motto to have No Regrets. Most days she could to stick to that directive easily, and this guy was annoying her. Which was also too bad. In another time and another place, she might have considered taking Officer Ballard for a spin.

But that was out of the question now.

"Adams-Larsen is a public relations firm. We specialize in high profile clients who need assistance with their public image."

"Clients no one can name," he shot back.

"Which is why we're very good at our job."

Before she could move in for the kill, he said, "So you're all about profit. It doesn't bother you at all that Beatrice Winter lied about who she is?"

Fortunately, Jill had very good control of her facial expressions and emotions. So she was more than confident that she hadn't given away her confusion. Because she might not be happy, but no way in hell was she going to give up a client to this guy.

"So you do care."

"I really have no idea what you're talking about." She lifted her chin.

"You're familiar with the America's Recovery Centers' case."

Of course she was familiar with it. Even though the Marshals had requested their help, ALIAS had also vetted Beatrice and done an in-depth background check on Ms. Winter before they'd agreed to do her relo. Marsh had overseen the case personally from start to finish, but he'd kept Jill apprised of the status.

Marsh had also disappeared not soon after Beatrice Winter's relocation was finalized.

But as far as Hamish Ballard was concerned, her only knowledge of the case was through the news. "I've seen some details in the news," she said noncommittally.

"Beatrice Winter turned in the company officials so she could get away with embezzling money from the company. And she was likely the one facilitating the supply of drugs to the patients while the sober houses and outpatient center were supposedly helping them with their addiction."

Jill's gut response was *No Fucking Way*.

But…crap on a cracker. Hamish Ballard seemed very convinced. What if that were true? Several of the center's patients had died. Not necessarily in the facility, but once they had been released, it hadn't taken long.

The Greek yogurt and strawberries she'd had for breakfast soured in the pit of her stomach. Was there any chance he was correct?

The upper management of the America's Recovery Centers who were charged in the case took plea deals, pleading guilty to Health Care Fraud. However, the government had never recovered the money. And they'd had forensic accountants looking. The CEO complained bitterly that paying lawyers for the lawsuit had depleted his funds to nothing. Supposedly he was broke. That was why he took the plea deal.

Boo fricking hoo.

The CFO had said, "Why would I embezzle the money? We were raking it in and had a good thing going. I was billing insurance companies hundreds of thousands of dollars a month and getting kickbacks from local referral centers and drug testing centers."

The government's response was "You knew the end was coming." There had been several high profile cases that ended in prison time for the perpetrators, and Florida was beginning to crack down on the "for profit" rehab centers.

This case was one in a long line of cases on the court dockets this year.

But no matter how hard the government searched, they hadn't been able to find the millions supposedly siphoned from the company's coffers. They were able to seize assets—cars, houses, planes from the executives—but the money was still missing.

Jill kept her face blank.

If there were a problem in her house, she would handle it. She didn't need Officer Hamish Blowhard Ballard interfering in ALIAS company business.

"Although we don't have any connection to Ms. Winter's case, I'm curious, how does this relate to an officer from...." She glanced at his austere card: A logo of the British crown, the agency, his name, and a cell phone number. "The National Crime Agency?"

"You didn't know about her, did you?" He narrowed his gaze.

"I have no idea what you mean, *Officer* Ballard."

If he were right, she was pissed. They had protocols in place. ALIAS's business model and company systems worked because they vetted their clients carefully. They were on the side of right, and everything they did was done legally, even if maybe sometimes they skimmed along the edge of legality. They had to maintain a careful and protected database of clients. Their clients' security was paramount. Media attention of any kind was not what ALIAS needed. Especially negative media attention.

The Marshals had vetted Beatrice before Dee had even passed her case on to ALIAS. No way was this guy right.

Ballard studied her shrewdly.

He seemed so sure that even though she didn't think there was anything wrong with Winter's case, she was certainly going to investigate. As soon as she got rid of him.

He strode right up to her desk, so close his thighs pressed against the edge. He slapped his palms on the burled mahogany. "If you won't give me the information or don't have the authority, then I want to speak to Marsh Adams."

How dare this arrogant fuck assume that she didn't have the knowledge or authority to run her own damn business? Unfortunately, his assumption was common. She'd put up with jackasses like him before.

"I am an equal partner and he isn't available," Jillian gritted out. She'd been the recipient of this kind of attitude before. People assumed she was merely a figurehead and didn't work at their business. Most days she ignored people who thought she was a placeholder, but this guy got under her skin. "And there is nothing to discuss. I'm sorry I can't help you find this woman."

He smiled, but it wasn't nice. It was the kind of smile she usually gave to people who she was about to eviscerate. And she didn't like it directed at her.

"I need to speak with Marsh Adams then."

It was good to have goals. She'd be happy to pawn this

douchenozzle off on her partner…if she had any freaking idea where Marsh was. But she could get rid of this guy by agreeing.

"Fine. He's out of range right now," she lied smoothly. "But as soon as he's available I'd be happy to put him in touch with you."

The smile disappeared. "I don't think you understand, Ms. Larsen." Ballard didn't move, but somehow he'd made his body bigger, more menacing. Neat trick. "If you don't give me his whereabouts, I will be returning with an international extradition order for Brianna Walsh aka Beatrice Winter with your name, Marsh Adams's name, and the firm of Adams-Larsen that will require you to turn her over."

Jill wanted to call his bluff. But on the off chance this asshole could get the paperwork, the implications for ALIAS would be bad and she didn't need any more bad press. So for now she had to play nice. She made her tone conciliatory. "Look. My partner is on sabbatical and I don't know if he's in cell range." She used her voice of diplomacy on him.

Dammit, Marsh.

"This is not a negotiable request." Ballard didn't back down. "I need to speak with him."

"I'll give him the message. But in the meantime, I have another appointment." She made a show of glancing at the Cartier tank watch on her wrist.

Don't let the door hit you in the ass was strongly implied.

Hamish Ballard, the bastard, huffed as if he knew she was lying about the appointment. But Jill hadn't lost her ability to read people, and something was off about I'm Officer Ballard and his bluster.

"You'll contact me when you hear from him?"

"Of course," Jill replied. "Adams-Larsen is always happy to cooperate with the authorities."

Authority or not, this guy was her enemy. A zealot was ten times more dangerous than a tenacious agent, and Hamish Ballard had *zealot* written all over him.

Chapter 2

------

ell, bollocks. That hadn't gone well at all.

W Hamish had intended to go in, charm the woman, and find out where Brianna Walsh aka Beatrice Winter was hiding. Instead he'd pissed off the best—and last—lead he had.

Jillian Larsen had pushed all his buttons. And instead of charming her, he'd lost his temper.

However, if he was any judge of character, she was going to be looking into his accusations straightaway. Hopefully he'd get the information he needed, even if it was through somewhat dodgy means.

He sauntered down the sidewalk away from the Adams-Larsen office. Jillian Larsen had been lying through her perfectly straight white teeth. Her "PR" agency had something to do with the disappearance of Brianna Walsh, the Irish mob princess.

Brianna's true nature extended back to her teen years growing up in one of the most notorious Irish crime families since the 60s. She'd been instrumental in putting her father and brothers away in exchange for a new identity and protection from her violent relatives. Except Hamish was convinced that she was actually worse than all her incarcerated relatives, and the ones still roaming free, combined.

She'd taken that new identity and fled to the United States. She could have disappeared and been safe. Instead, she became the self-ascribed whistleblower of a big scandal in the US medical industry and then proceeded to testify against the executives on trial.

Hamish had studied everything about Brianna Walsh, he knew her, and he knew that she was going to continue her criminal ways. She'd already started. But Hamish wasn't going to let her get away with it, and he was going to get vengeance for his brother if it was the last thing he did.

The path to vengeance started with Adams-Larsen and its founder Jillian. There was something rotten at Adams-Larsen, and Hamish was going to find out what it was. Because he knew that the agency was the key to finding Brianna and getting justice for his brother.

The first step had been put in motion by his visit.

He had to hope that Jillian Larsen didn't regularly sweep for bugs. He'd planted two listening devices in her office. One when he'd been sitting in the chair and the other when he'd loomed over her desk.

He headed back to his Airbnb, within walking distance of her office, to listen in on Jillian Larsen's office goings-on. After business hours were over, he'd check out Marsh Adams's apartment. Because her reaction to his query about her partner was suspicious.

She hadn't liked his intimation about her status one bit.

Maybe if hadn't insinuated that she was merely a figurehead, he'd have gotten further. Although from his research that was what he had assumed.

And while he thought he'd been able to read her—she'd been pissed—he still wasn't sure if she was involved in a criminal way, or if she and her partner had been hoodwinked by Brianna.

But he didn't give a shite.

His stomach rolled. Adams-Larsen was the last lead he had left. He was on the edge of getting the boot. And if his boss had any idea he'd come across the pond to pursue the lead on Brianna Walsh, he'd be sacked for sure. Since Jillian Larsen had refused to give up Brianna's location when she clearly knew the woman, she was his enemy.

Bugger.

The bugs had to pay off.

He shoved aside the desperation that dogged him. He'd hoped that the disgraced former US Marshal now owner of Adams-Larsen would cave and answer his questions when she discovered that Brianna was a criminal.

The only way to make Brianna pay for her crimes was to find her.

Brianna had managed to fool the British authorities, and he'd bet that she'd fooled Jillian Larsen as well. But the fact that Jillian had refused to even discuss Brianna had put his back up.

Jillian Larsen hadn't been what he'd expected. He'd dug into his research on the plane and on paper she'd come across as a slightly irresponsible formal marshal who had somehow managed to land on her feet and salvage a career from the train wreck of an op gone horribly wrong. He'd assumed that she would be an easy mark and she'd give up her intelligence on Brianna aka Beatrice without a fight. After all, her lax standards had been the death of her key witness in a criminal trial—although she'd managed to keep him alive to testify.

But now Hamish had questions.

She exuded sophistication and competence. Her slim pencil skirt and fitted blouse evoked a sort of 50s fashion style. Her perfect lipstick, a bold in-your-face red, accented her lush mouth, portraying a sexy airhead. But in a startling contrast, her smooth facial expressions hid a cunning, secretive woman. She hadn't given away a thing.

Nothing he'd said had seemed to rattle her.

Jillian Larsen had left US Marshals in disgrace. The exact details of her exit were shrouded in mystery.

Brianna Walsh aka Beatrice Winter was responsible for the death of his brother. She might not have pressed the plunger on his syringe, but she'd been his pusher. If only Hamish had figured it out sooner. But he'd left his brother's meager belongings packed in boxes. And when Hamish could finally bear to read Charlie's journal, a practice that his rehab center had insisted on as part of his treatment, Hamish had discovered that Brianna was actually encouraging the inhabitants of the rehab center to do drugs. She had offered Charlie drugs several times.

His brother had overdosed in rehab. And Hamish was going to make Brianna pay.

Bringing her down would likely only assuage his guilt because his brother was never coming back.

But maybe, just maybe, he'd find some peace.

ONCE HAMISH RETURNED to his flat, he set up to listen in on Jillian's conversations.

He shifted on the small hard sofa, his thoughts returning to their meeting. His body had reacted to hers with a surprising, sexual enthusiasm. That moment when they'd shaken hands was burned into his temporal lobe. No doubt. But he wasn't about to be swayed by pretty face, he wasn't some rookie on his first assignment.

Was Marsh Adams the key?

Jillian Larsen's very slight reaction had given her away. He might not have even noticed if he hadn't been intently staring at her, but her gray eyes had flickered, and he had seen that initial moment of shock. Could tell that she hadn't known about Brianna's past. But ignorance was not a defense. At the root of the mystery of Brianna's location was the Adams-Larsen Inc. and Associates public relations firm. It had taken a month of investigation, illegal use of the NCA's databases, and ultimately a favor from a friend at MI5 to track her to Florida where she worked for America's Recovery Centers and then to Adams-Larsen in Washington.

When Jillian had shifted gears and shared that her partner was on sabbatical, he knew he was on the right track.

He could only pray that the small, hopefully undetectable bugs planted in her office would start feeding him intel right away.

Aye, he'd broken the rules. Aye, he'd get in trouble if he was caught. And anything he heard would not hold up in a court of law but at this point he just needed to find Brianna, and he only had a week to do it.

He loosened his tie, took off his shoes, notched the headphones in his ear and settled in with a wee dram of scotch and a paper and pen.

Fortunately, he didn't have long to wait.

"Maria! I need this client file." She rattled off a reference number and Hamish dutifully wrote it in his notebook. "And I need it pronto."

Jillian Larsen's husky voice echoed in his ear, his cock chubbing at the trigger. "Show our trainee how to find files."

As he waited for the receptionist, a Latina woman, to deliver the files, anticipation washed over him. Could it really be this easy?

"Umm, Jill?"

He'd been so lost in the fantasy of slapping handcuffs on Brianna, he jolted when he heard the secretary's hesitant voice.

"Come on in."

The door closed softly.

"Have you got the file for me?" Her throaty voice continued to cause an unexpected physical reaction. Hamish shifted on the sofa.

They weren't even in the same room and she was affecting him. He needed to shut that down straightaway.

"Umm, that's what I wanted to talk to you about."

"What's wrong?"

"There is no file."

"That's…not possible."

"I triple checked." Her voice was hesitant. "I couldn't find anything under that number."

Jillian's keyboard clacked in his ear. "Try these numbers." She rattled off two more numbers and Hamish wrote those down as well.

After another few minutes, the receptionist came back. "I pulled those files for you."

"Thanks." Jillian dismissed the woman. "Can you send Viktor to my office?"

"Sure." The door closed.

He could hear the flipping of papers and then the thump when she dumped them back on her desk.

The clack of the computer keys echoed in his ear. She

exhaled sharply, then muttered, "Dammit, Marsh. Why is the info on Beatrice Winter gone?"

Ha, he'd been right. They had had contact with Brianna. Did they have something to do with her disappearance? He surely hoped so.

He gripped his pen tightly and waited.

The beep of cell buttons being pushed was soft and indistinct. Her fingers drummed in his ear.

After a minute, she said, "Marsh. It's time. I need you to call me back. There's a guy here asking questions about Beatrice Winter. Saying she's a criminal. And I need your input."

He listened to her curse softly after she hung up the phone.

While the words weren't a complete indication that they knew where she was, it was a step in the right direction.

JILLIAN WAITED for Viktor to close the door to her office.

"You wanted to see me, boss?"

"Yes." Jill stared at the stripped contents of the file on Beatrice Winter. "You worked phase one of the Winter case, correct?"

He sat down gingerly. "Yes."

He seemed anxious, not what she intended him to feel. She studied Viktor, wondering what was going on with him.

"Is there a problem?" he finally asked.

"Not at all." Look at her, becoming a champion liar. "I wondered if you have had a chance to test the results."

Misinformation, obscuring the details of a client's life, took time and a meticulous attention to detail.

"Marsh took care of it."

Marsh again. Huh. What the hell, Marsh?

"Can you double test what he did?"

"Absolutely. It won't take long. She was pretty light on accounts."

"Light?"

"Yeah. Besides utilities, apartment, and one credit card, she didn't really have customer accounts. She was a one step removed from completely off the grid."

"No grocery affiliate points or iTunes or Amazon or pharmacy points?"

"Nope." Viktor shook his head. "She seemed to have an almost pathological lack of accounts."

Or…she had a brand spanking new identity and hadn't had time to sign up for anything. Jill's suspicions were growing. Dammit.

"Can you do an audit and get back to me with the results?"

"Sure thing." He released a soft, sad breath and stood up. He walked without his usual efficiency, his movements slow, as if he was wading through the sadness that surrounded him.

Jill always tried to straddle that line between being interested in her employees and not invading their privacy. But she also thought of herself like their mother. Adams-Larsen was her family and she was the matriarch. Which was ironic, since she hadn't seen her mother in thirty years. "Anything else bothering you?"

Viktor shrugged. "I'm fine."

Fine. Possibly the most ambiguous word in the English language. Fine did not mean fine.

"Do you…want to talk about the breakup?" she asked softly, somewhat dreading the answer. She wanted to help, but she had no idea if she could.

Please say no. Please say no. Please say no.

Viktor paused, looked at her. "Not sure there's much to talk about. It's over. And basically, I need to move on."

But clearly he wasn't moving on. At least not yet. So instead of talking, Jill listened.

In the weight of that silence, Viktor's eyes sheened. "I thought he was the one." He curled his fingers into a fist.

The one. She didn't know what to say. Honestly, she pretty much believed *the one* was a myth. Although lately her friends were convinced they had found that elusive *one* and seemed incredibly happy.

What would it be like? To find that one person who completed you? Years ago she had believed Dominic might be the one. But she'd been wrong. Now she wasn't a big believer in the concept. But after watching Bliss and Jack, Marissa and John, Kita and Alex, and even Dwayne and Maria, she thought she didn't have a fucking clue.

"Sometimes…" She started, then stopped. "Sometimes we just have to keep moving. It gets easier." And it did get easier. And still she felt the inadequacy of her words in his small smile.

"Thanks, Jill."

Another moment when she needed Marsh. He was the far more touchy-feely of the two of them. If she was the matriarch, Marsh was the patriarch. Together they tended their small flock of employees.

Sure she was an emotionally stunted, physically unavailable mother but still. Marsh always took care of dispensing fist bumps and back-slapping hugs. But Marsh wasn't here.

She thought about it for a minute. What would Marsh do?

"Do you…need a hug?" She felt stupid because her first instinct was to step away from intimacy.

"That would be nice," he replied softly.

Jillian set her coffee cup on her desk and tentatively wrapped her arms around his shoulders. Viktor curved his arms around her waist, the hug still slightly awkward, that lean in without really touching, except maybe the cheek and neck.

"It will get better," she whispered in his ear. "But maybe go see if Kita will let you kick the shit out of her."

"Great idea."

"Have her dress up in the mugger outfit and we can put a printout of your ex's face over the hood."

Viktor laughed, his shoulder shaking.

"If that doesn't work, go out and get drunk."

Viktor laughed again, this time a little heartier. "Thanks, boss." He left her office with a little more spring in his step and an actual smile on his face.

Her sense of accomplishment was out of proportion to the small success. But she'd take the win anyway.

JILL PUNCHED in numbers on her phone and waited as it rang on the other end of line. She connected with Dee's admin, a very grumpy gatekeeper who put her through to her old boss and mentor.

"Deanna Womack."

"Dee, it's Jill." Jill pressed her hand flat on top of the nearly empty file. "I need to talk to you about a case that you referred to us a few months ago."

"Ask away." As if Dee wasn't quite paying attention.

"I really believe this needs to be discussed in person."

There was silence on the other end of the phone. Jill heard the soft exhale from her former boss. She had to know exactly who Jill was talking about because…there had only been one case recently.

"I'm busy today." Dee paused again as if consulting her calendar. "I can see you tomorrow morning, say ten a.m."

"Ten tomorrow morning is perfect." Jill frowned at the flat tone of Dee's voice. "See you then."

What in the fresh hell was going on?

A strange man asking about Beatrice Winter. Most of the contents of the main file missing. Viktor's comment about Beatrice's unconnected life. Dee not even flinching to schedule a meeting as if she already knew there were discrepancies regarding Beatrice Winter.

Years ago, Deanna Womack had had Jill's back. But that telltale exhale when Jill asked for the meeting had alarm bells ringing everywhere. Dee could have resisted a face-to-face if she deemed the information wasn't too sensitive, but she hadn't argued about meeting in person. Based on the intel Hamish Ballard had just shoved down her throat, that lack of hesitation was doubly concerning.

A knock on the door interrupted her musings.

Kita bounced into Jill's office in spandex shorts and a wicking tank top. She threw herself into the chair across from Jill's desk and propped her chin on her fist. "So what was up with the Scottish Hottie?"

Jill snorted. "Scottish pain in my ass, you mean."

"Sure." She smirked.

Jill didn't intend to confide in Kita, especially due to the sensitive nature of his accusations. "He was just here as a courtesy while here tracking down a suspect."

"Someone we know?" Kita asked.

"No one important," Jill lied again. It was time to start

delving into Marsh's privacy. "Say, can you do me a favor and give me a list of all of Marsh's credit card charges from the beginning of his hiatus."

Kita sat straight up in the chair, blinked. "You want me to illegally hack Marsh's bank account?"

Jill laughed nervously. "Of course not." She tapped her fingernails on those empty files again. She might not be interested in helping Hamish Ballard. And she might not want to keep looking for Marsh. He needed to come home on his own. But it certainly wouldn't hurt to review and trace his locations after he did his disappearing act.

"I'm talking about his company credit card charges."

Kita sank back into the cushy chair. "Oh, darn. I was hoping for a little illegal hacking." Her eyes sparkled with mischief and she gave a devilish little laugh. "Kidding."

Jill fought the urge to smooth her hair down when she knew it was already perfect. Because Kita had planted the seed. What if she had Kita hack Marsh's private transactions as well?

She was floundering, wondering if Beatrice Winter really was Brianna Walsh, wondering if her partner had known that something was off with their client. Damn Hamish Ballard for even putting that thought in her head. But now that it was there, it worried away at the recesses of her brain. What if Beatrice really was a criminal? What if Marsh wasn't missing, but he'd followed her or she'd done something to him?

Jill knew that Marsh and Beatrice had had a sexual relationship. Jill certainly couldn't throw stones, since the whole reason ALIAS existed was because of her ill-advised relationship with a witness she had protected. What she did know…Hamish Ballard was a threat to ALIAS, their employees, and their clients. And if he kept pushing, a threat to her. She needed all the ammunition she could get to head him off and make this go away.

Because if he kept digging, if he kept poking at Jill and demanding answers, someone was bound to take notice.

Kita tilted her head. "I thought we'd decided not to look for Marsh."

She had…until a certain Scottish officer exploded into her office and thrown around accusations that Jill couldn't let stand.

"On second thought—" Jill avoided Kita's inquisitive gaze "—can you get Marsh's personal transactions as well?"

Kita was no longer smiling, because she understood the implications of what Jill was asking. "You sure?"

"Yes."

"What's going on?"

"I'm not at liberty to discuss it."

"But—"

Jill held up her palm because even though she was asking Kita for something illegal, she didn't want to say the words out loud. "We understand each other?"

"I'm on it, boss." Kita headed for the door, turned around, grabbed the knob and gave Jill one last measuring look. "You know what you're doing?"

No fucking clue. But wasn't that how you got through life sometimes? Fake it until you make it. "Yes."

"You know I'm your friend."

"I know." They were sort of friends.

A pang of envy hit Jill. Because Kita had been Marsh's friend first, and Jill couldn't afford to overlook the fact that if Kita had to choose between Jill and Marsh…that Marsh would win hands down. Kita was a bit of a rule breaker. She didn't hesitate when the safety or reputation of someone she cared about was on the line. Which meant that Jill couldn't confide in Kita. She was all alone.

Jill had to be loyal to the entire company. Their clients and her employees. Kita was passionate and committed, but she would break the rules in a hot minute to protect Marsh.

Chapter 3

Hamish listened for another two hours until Jillian Larsen left for the day, but she hadn't said anything else that would be considered incriminating. Or lead him to his prey.

Hamish closed his laptop and headed out the door. Time to check out Marsh Adams's condominium. Based on the message Jillian left on Marsh's cell, Hamish thought Marsh might be gone, out of town. So maybe that sabbatical she'd blown him off with was real. Marsh definitely hadn't called her back while Hamish was listening.

Thirty minutes later, Hamish was casing the exterior of the eight-story brick building with a delivery ramp in the back and doorman at the front entrance. Cameras mounted on each of the corners and lights on the back were more for security than attractive illumination.

He studied the people going in and out, waiting for the right opportunity, until finally he saw a pizza delivery van pull in behind the building.

He sidled up to the van as the delivery person was getting out. "Hello, mate."

"*Dios*, you scared me." The skinny, young Hispanic kid put a hand to his chest.

"Hey, I want to surprise my girlfriend." He patted his pocket; he'd brought a small box that would look like a ring box as a precaution. "Could I deliver that for you?"

The kid held the pizza box in front of him like a shield, his fingers tightening as if Hamish was going to steal the pie. "I can't do that. If you stole the pizza, I'd be fired."

"You can watch me go in the elevator." Hamish put his hand over his heart. "I promise I will make your delivery."

He reached into his wallet and pulled out several twenty US bills. "You would be helping me out." He gave the kid a conspiratorial grin. "She's hacked off at me and I need to make a grand gesture. But she won't let me in." He patted the box again.

The kid's eyes lit up at the money. He reached for the cash.

"Can I borrow the hat too?"

"How much money is that?"

"A hundred US."

"US?"

"Dollars."

"Sure," he said enthusiastically. "I've got another hat."

"Thanks mate, I owe you." Hamish got the address of the apartment that ordered the pizza. "I promise I'll deliver it."

"Good luck with your girl," the kid called out.

For one brief moment, a picture of Jillian Larsen flashed in Hamish's mind. He wouldn't mind a girl like that. With her smoky voice and sultry lips and yet all buttoned up, she was totally lush. A temptation—if he'd been here under any other circumstances, he'd have chatted her up and hoped for a date. Or one night in a posh hotel. But she wasn't for him.

Get your head out of your arse and get cracking.

He headed into the building and nodded briefly at the doorman. "Pizza for 5A."

"Go on up."

Hamish took the elevator and delivered the pizza quickly, brushing aside the tip. "Give it to the guy next time."

As soon as the tenant shut their door, he hustled to the stairwell. Within minutes he was on the top floor of the grand old building. All the other floors had eight condominiums but this floor only had two.

Hamish slipped a set of lockpicks out of his pocket and jiggled the lock on 8B. The well-oiled lock took some finesse, but he was able to slip inside within sixty seconds.

The apartment was dark since November's short days meant night had fallen, but ambient light from the full moon filtered through the curtainless windows. He slipped on a pair of cheap vinyl gloves, then pulled out his cell phone and used the flashlight app to shine some light on the sparsely decorated bachelor pad. Hamish moved with precision through the apartment, opening drawers and searching for any clue to help him find Marsh Adams.

He'd just begun to search the closet when the sound of the lock turning caught his ear.

Shite.

Hamish shut off the light and ducked underneath the row of hanging suits to settle in.

He wanted to hear what Marsh Adams was up to before he confronted the guy. So much for Jillian Larsen's assertion that she couldn't reach her partner.

Keys clanked on the metal kitchen table with a loud thud. Cabinet doors opened and shut, as if the bloke was looking for something rather than getting dinner.

The sounds continued getting progressively louder as Adams made his way to the bedroom. Except as the sound of muttering hit his ears, Hamish realized that it *wasn't* Adams.

The voice was female, breathy, and his body recognized her before his brain.

His cock had stiffened and his heartbeat picked up as Jillian Larsen's distinctive rasp rubbed over his nerve endings.

"Where the hell are you, Marsh?" A dresser drawer slammed. "This is a waste of time."

Hamish ducked farther beneath the suits and hoped that her search path wasn't the same as his. He was too big to really be concealed beneath the clothing. If she turned on the closet light, she'd see him for sure. Shoes, suits, even socks and underwear were neatly lined up in the meticulously ordered walk-in closet. He shifted carefully until he was behind the path of the door. If she opened it and didn't look behind the door, there was a chance she wouldn't see him. But if she walked all the way into the closet, he was done for.

If there were something in Marsh Adams's apartment, Hamish hadn't had a chance to find it. And she didn't seem to be having any better luck.

Give up, go home, he mentally chanted as she muttered while opening and closing drawers.

But of course his luck wasn't that good. Wasn't that the way of it?

The closet door shoved open so hard that even though he'd been anticipating just this situation, the door hit him in the head. Normally closet doors opened outward but again, just his luck this one had opened inward.

"Oomph." He muffled a soft grunt, trying but unable to

completely stifle the noise. Which was probably for the best. If he'd caught her completely unaware then she might have shot first asked questions later. Americans.

"What the hell?"

Hamish shook his head to clear it and stood swiftly.

He wasn't sure what was more disorienting…the scent of her perfume wafting to him or the hit he'd taken to his face.

"Hands where I can see them." Jillian had backed away from him—aye, the closet was that damn big. She held a large revolver in a two-handed grip, her expression fierce, intense.

He slowly raised his hands and then lifted his lips into his best charming grin. "Fancy seeing you here."

"Ballard?" Her hard frown faltered.

He bowed. "At your service."

"What the hell are you doing in my partner's closet?"

JILL COULDN'T COMPUTE.

Why was Hamish Ballard in Marsh's condo? The annoying, uptight agent from this afternoon had disappeared. He wore casual skinny jeans and a navy wool sweater. His lopsided smile and self-deprecating manner were contrasted by the shocking trail of blood running down his face from the rapidly swelling cut above his right navy eye.

"I'm guessin' the same as you." His hands began to lower slowly.

"Keep 'em up." She gestured with her weapon. He was a little too close to her if he decided to attack. Deadliest distance in a gunfight was three to six feet. If he had a weapon, he didn't even need to be a good shot to kill her. She didn't actually think he was dangerous—to her—but she'd been wrong before.

Even with the lump and the blood, his sexuality filled up the large closet, wrapping around her with a surprising intensity. His raw-boned attractiveness was enhanced by a current of electricity that thrummed beneath the surface of their interaction. Her hormones sure picked the wrong day to wake up from hibernation.

And definitely the wrong guy.

She'd never been with a man who hadn't respected her and she wasn't about to start now. And why the *hell* was she thinking about being with a man?

She gestured to the open doorway and said abruptly, "We need to talk."

"I'd prefer to do so without a firearm in my face." But he didn't take his gaze from hers.

"Don't do anything wrong and I won't shoot you."

He laughed. "Fair enough."

"Go on."

He hesitated, glancing between the weapon and her eyes, then he turned his back on her and walked out into Marsh's bedroom.

Jill tucked her weapon into the holster at her waist and followed him. He headed into the open concept living room and kitchen area.

He opened the fridge and rummaged around, dumping ice cubes into a Ziplock bag. Then he wrapped the bag in a dishtowel and pressed the makeshift ice pack to his swelling cut.

"You're awfully comfortable with breaking and entering." Her suspicion meter was off the charts. Why would he break into Marsh's home?

"I could say the same of you," he replied blandly. But he didn't deny the B&E comment. This guy was not conforming to her expectations. At all.

"I have a key."

"Good for you." He took the ice cubes from his forehead and frowned at the blood on the towel.

"You want to tell me what you're doing in my partner's home?"

He eyed her, his marbled blue gaze sweeping up and down her body with sizzling intensity. "You more than partners?"

Jill bristled. Why was it that everything always came down to whether she was sleeping with someone? Or not? It wasn't any of his fucking business. Thanks to her reputation, she got asked that question a lot more than she'd like. But she had saved Dominic even if the only people who knew were Marsh and Dee, so a hit to her rep had been worth it in the end.

"Answer the damn question." She tightened her mouth and waited.

He sighed. "I was looking for clues as to his whereabouts."

"Why?"

He hesitated. "Why won't you tell me where he is?"

She didn't want to notice his sculpted jaw or muscled chest. And she definitely didn't want to wonder what his body would feel like pressed up against hers. He was trying to appear nonthreatening but it wasn't working.

Hamish Ballard was a predator. Sure he hid it beneath that boyish demeanor and somewhat charming accent but she saw through that act, and no way was she going to let him in or let him know that Marsh was missing—along with most of the file on their client. Not that she'd admitted that Beatrice was a client. She'd never betray her mission.

She needed to get rid of this guy so she could continue searching Marsh's apartment, looking for any kind of clue to where he might have gone. "Because it isn't any of your business."

"You don't know where he is, do you?" He straightened. "That's what you meant."

"I don't know what you're talking about, but it's time for you to leave." He was lucky she didn't call the cops. But she couldn't. Reporters in DC were always looking at police records and blotters for scandal tips. Because of an incident at ALIAS a few months ago, the agency was on the reporters' radar.

A fugitive broke into their offices, held a hostage, and died in a shoot-out. Unfortunately, that situation had made the papers. Unavoidable.

"You don't want any publicity," Hamish shot back after a pause.

Ugh, the guy had a point. They didn't need any more bad publicity and if he went on record and made noise he could make life difficult for her. Protecting their clients was imperative.

Instead of obeying her and leaving, he said, "I tracked Brianna Walsh, your Beatrice Winter, to Adams-Larsen."

Impossible.

She could admire his tenacity even while she wanted to kick him in the balls. "I told you before that we don't have any information on her."

Because it was all buried and hidden. *Protect the client.*

And yet she couldn't afford to piss off the National Crime Agency. So she'd have to play nice, sort of.

But what Jill didn't get was how Beatrice Winter had

managed to get such good documents and forms of ID if she was actually a British citizen. Viktor's assessment came back to her.

"Why are you so invested in finding this woman?"

Because his attitude and determination were excessive for an officer looking for a single criminal. She could appreciate his dedication to the mission, but his intensity struck her as overzealous.

"She's wanted back home."

"That's not the only reason. You're way too aggressive about tracking down this woman. You committed unlawful entry by breaking in here. I could have you arrested."

"Doubtful." But his gaze narrowed in displeasure and something else. A glimmer of alarm?

Jill's bullshit meter perked up. This guy wasn't on the up and up.

"Look, I only want to speak with your partner."

She crossed her arms and leaned against the shiny, rarely used granite countertops. "And I told you that I would have him call you. That hardly seems to warrant breaking and entering."

She'd been right before. He was a zealot.

And zealots were dangerous.

"I'm impatient," he drawled.

Jillian rolled her eyes. Really? That was his explanation? "I'll get back to you."

"If I don't hear from you, I'll have to go public," Hamish said. "Do you really want me going on record asking questions about your client?"

"She isn't a client." Not anymore.

Maybe if she denied it enough he would finally believe her.

"I read about your agency, you know."

About *you* was implied.

"Congratulations! You can read!"

He snorted. "What really happened with your protectee before you left the US Marshals?"

No one had ever asked her that before.

The official story was that she'd had an affair with a protectee, and her protectee had died, killed by the organization he'd testified against to send a message to anyone else who thought ratting out the bosses and the organization was a good idea. As a consequence, she'd gotten kicked out. Of course, it was much more complicated than that.

"He's gone."

"I'm aware of that." He tilted his head, and the light from over the kitchen table cast shadows along his sharply defined jaw.

No one but she, Marsh, and Dee knew that Dominic was still alive. Everyone thought she'd carelessly used her position to have sex with a protectee. And that her negligent actions had caused him to die.

And none of that information was referenced in the ALIAS company marketing materials. So he'd clearly dug deep, and not in official channels, to find info about ALIAS.

She glanced away from his penetrating stare.

How had he managed to turn this around on her? She was off and out of sorts. Clearly.

"But that's not all to the story." He made the statement as if he knew her. That was tantalizing—her own father had believed that she'd willfully neglected the safety of her charge. He hadn't spoken to her since the event that had changed her life and sent her on a new path.

She stayed silent.

"I can read between the lines."

When she looked at him, she saw an unexpected understanding in his gaze. She wanted to trust him, and she longed to confide in someone.

She missed Marsh. He was her touchstone. The one person who knew her well enough that he could stop the doubts and insecurities that occasionally plagued her.

And she was lonely.

Which was no excuse for letting down her guard in front of this stranger. Life had kicked her in the ass one too many times. But she'd risen every time, dusted herself off and moved on.

No regrets.

A pretty face wasn't going to convince her to relax from a lifetime of guarding her secrets. He was the enemy even if her body wanted him to be her ally.

"There are no lines." She hardened her resolve, racking her brain for anything that might give her a clue as to where Marsh was located. She'd had people looking for him. Checking out his other homes. But it was as if he'd completely disappeared.

If he hadn't sent her a note, encrypted with their secret code right after he'd left, then she might have tipped over from annoyance to worry about foul play.

She usually didn't mind him taking time off. After all, his reputation had taken a severe hit when he'd quit the Marshals and opened ALIAS with her. They'd both been disenchanted with the system, but Marsh could have stayed and had a stellar career. He'd been on track to make supervisor before all the stuff with Dominic went down.

Marsh continually insisted that he was perfectly happy, but she didn't want him to ever regret leaving the Marshals to found ALIAS. So she mostly shrugged philosophically when he did his little walkabouts. Except he'd been gone much longer this time, and no one had been able to reach him.

Jill frowned.

Marsh, where are you?

His apartment was a bust. Her neatnik partner hadn't left any giant clues strewn around his place.

Jill ignored Hamish Ballard and studied the kitchen. A trio of houseplants in matching pots decorated the bay window. The leaves were dried and half dead.

Half dead as if someone had watered them. Marsh? Or maybe Kita had come by after Jillian had confessed last month that Marsh hadn't been in contact for a while.

Had he been back?

His laptop was missing. They never brought any work files home. Their client files and information were too sensitive. Each client was identified by a number. No names in the files. And the naming convention was a complicated algorithm so that if anyone broke into their system, they'd be unable to connect their client names with their current locations. Jill fortunately had a facility for numbers and for some reason, Beatrice's file number had stuck with her.

But most of Beatrice Winter's file was missing. And so was Marsh. Maybe he'd discovered that Beatrice had lied to them. But why go off on his own? That didn't make any sense. They were partners.

Her first responsibility was always to the client. Marsh too. So maybe he was trying to protect Beatrice? But if so, why would he disappear? Between their clients and their employees, ALIAS was her life. And she would do anything to protect it.

All she wanted was to find Marsh and ask him what the hell was going on.

She tapped her index finger on her mouth.

Nothing made sense.

HAMISH STUDIED JILLIAN.

So many layers beneath that uptight exterior. His instincts had been spot on. There was a hell of a lot more to the story about her exit from the US Marshals than what was public knowledge. But when she literally shut down before his eyes, he knew she wasn't going to share with him.

It wasn't germane to his investigation. This trip was about avenging his brother, not discovering the secrets of one prickly ex-US Marshal.

He forced his thoughts back to Brianna Walsh and Marsh Adams. Hamish had a feeling if he could find Marsh, then Brianna would be nearby.

Because although she hadn't admitted it, Hamish was pretty sure that Marsh Adams had disappeared. Based on the phone call he'd heard earlier today and the fact that she'd been in her partner's apartment looking for information, her actions were a big fucking clue.

She didn't know where Marsh Adams was.

But pushing her on that wasn't going to garner her cooperation. He was smoother than that. Even if he hadn't displayed those smarts up to now.

What was it about Jillian Larsen that caused him to throw away his common sense? And lose his innate charm?

His head throbbed where she'd accidentally hit him, but the ache went deeper. Adams-Larsen was his last lead. If this didn't pan out, he had no intelligence left to pursue. He couldn't let the woman who killed his brother roam free. And he had limited time to make this happen. If his boss found out he'd disobeyed a direct order to drop "this career-killing search" for Brianna Walsh, he was in deep shit. She'd threatened to sack him. *Get on with your fuckin' life, Ham.*

But he couldn't just get on with his life as if this case wasn't personal.

He owed it to his brother and to every future victim of the unconscionable criminal who pretended to want to help drug addicts and then fed their addiction at a very high price.

If he could just catch Brianna, bring her to justice, then he'd find some relief from the unrelenting guilt. He should have checked in on his brother. Should have understood that the addiction that had gripped him in its talons was back.

But he'd been busy, chasing down criminals, pursuing a promotion at the National Crime Agency with the cyber crimes division, and tracking down criminals in the cyber world—mostly safe in his office. So obsessed with random criminals that he hadn't seen the malevolent evil lurking in his brother's life.

"I just want to ask him some questions." He tried to cajole, but his voice was heavy with grief, and the desperation that was never far from the surface shone through his plea. "Can't you get me in touch with him?"

Marsh Adams was her partner. She should know where he might be. He didn't get a dishonest vibe from her, but that didn't matter. If she wouldn't share her information, she was his enemy.

Of course, Hamish's boss had no idea where he was, so it was entirely possible that Jillian Larsen didn't know where her partner was.

"I would if I could, just so we could clear up this misunderstanding." She smiled craftily.

And Hamish was on guard again. Now she was planning on lying to him. He'd let her distract him from his initial assessment, but no more. Jillian Larsen was not his friend or his ally.

Maybe he was looking at this all wrong.

"Why would Marshall Adams leave to start a PR firm with you?"

She stiffened; her smile didn't falter but Hamish scanned the kitchen for loose knives, just in case. And shit, he was getting a boner. The fact that she was dangerous should *not* be a turn-on.

"I'll have Marsh call you as soon as I hear from him."

Who was this smiling, accommodating woman brushing him off with a fake smile? Not the business owner in her office. Not the concerned partner on the phone. Not the patient boss with her hurting employee. Even at her kindest, she never used that sweet tone with anyone. He wasn't falling for it.

Then Jillian did a complete about-face, throwing him off-kilter again. "Hypothetically if she was a client…I would be unable to comment on her situation."

"So you admit she's a client." Not exactly what she said.

She blinked slowly, not giving anything away. "What is she allegedly wanted for?"

Allegedly? He bristled. "Did they ever find the money?"

She grabbed the bag of ice and dumped it in the sink. "Are you referring to the money that the rehab center executives pocketed?"

"*Allegedly* pocketed." He tossed the legal term right back at her.

She rolled her eyes. "The money is missing."

"The executives didn't take the money," Hamish said fiercely. "She did."

"There was absolutely no evidence that she had the skills

or the access to steal that money," she shot back, clearly annoyed.

"Then you Yanks missed it." Hamish knew. Brianna'd been cleaned out when she'd left Britain. The deal for her testimony was no jail time and a new identity with resettlement. All the family's cash had been confiscated by the government. If she had offshore accounts or cash stashed away, they hadn't been able to find them. "She nicked the cash."

If he could find her bank accounts, then he'd have her. But he needed at least some sort of jumping-off point. And Jillian Larsen was the only lead he had.

He'd do anything to find Brianna Walsh and bring her to justice. And he'd expose Jillian Larsen for the fraud she was.

She might continue to deny being involved with Brianna but her verbal slipup a minute ago revealed that she did know more than she was saying.

But he could play nice for now and pretend to work with her until it was time to take them all down.

She'd helped hide a criminal. Helped hide the woman responsible for his brother's death.

He wasn't going to forget that.

But he'd use her, and her resources, without compunction. Even if he could sense the conflict within her.

She was a means to an end, nothing more.

Chapter 4

The lump on Hamish's head was turning purple, and a small smear of blood lingered over his eyebrow.

Jill winced mentally. Oops.

Protect ALIAS at all costs. But to protect Adams-Larsen she needed to find her partner.

She retrieved a dishtowel from one of the kitchen drawers, one she'd given Marsh if she wasn't mistaken, and dampened half of it so she could clean him up. Because she couldn't stand to see that trickle of blood on his face.

She didn't trust him. But she needed to use him and his information about Beatrice.

However Jill couldn't appear too eager to collaborate with Hamish. He'd suspect she was up to something. That was part of the reason she'd been so flippant a second ago. She wanted him off that line of questioning.

She wanted to do some more digging into Beatrice and the missing money and every other thing that suddenly seemed off about their client.

Her first responsibility was to the client, second, the agency. But if Hamish Ballard was telling the truth, then their client had fraudulently represented herself and she might even be guilty of bigger crimes, potentially stealing the money from the drug rehab centers.

If they had inadvertently helped a criminal evade justice, she would be first in line to take the woman down. But *quietly*.

Hamish Ballard sat at the small table, his elbow on the edge. He blinked when she flipped on the light hanging over the clear glass tabletop.

She peered at his lump and then wiped at the small smear of blood, her touch gentle. His shoulders loosened, rounded, and his eyes drifted shut.

And Jill was suddenly aware of his shoulders. Wide and bulky, they filled the space between her and the table. He wasn't particularly tall, but his broad chest and solid form were a somehow comforting presence.

When she stepped closer, her body responded to his. Her pulse tripped at his nearness. Goose bumps cascaded over her skin at the soft puff of his breath against her neck. The air between them heated, thickened.

Jill inhaled, trying to ignore their sizzling attraction even as her body overruled her brain. If her hormones were in charge, she'd be jumping him right now.

She sighed. Because that wasn't going to happen.

His eyes opened, the blue darkening to a sexy navy. He grabbed her wrist as she bent over.

"What are you doing?' His fingers were firm around her wrist, not too tight but unyielding.

His scent heated the chilly air. Pine—like the aroma of Christmas, holidays, and the longing for family—surrounded her. She shoved away that fanciful thought. Jillian Larsen didn't do fanciful.

She was tough, formidable, not the type of woman who

emanated softness. She'd had years to perfect her outer shell. She took no shit and she followed her own code.

She stared at his fingers around her wrist.

Grown men quivered in fear when she turned her assessing stare on them.

Just because she'd been tried and convicted in the court of public opinion about her conduct when she'd left the Marshals didn't mean that she'd dropped her standards. She'd been raised to have an unshakeable core of ethics and a strong moral compass. And she hadn't deviated off course.

"Cleaning you up." Her voice was even and seemingly unaffected, but it took work.

Completely out of character for her. She didn't have a nurturing bone in her body, and she figured adults could take care of themselves. But she had the overwhelming urge to tend to him.

"You're taking care of me?"

"Yes," she said through gritted teeth. "Is that so strange?"

"You don't seem like the type."

Yeah, she wasn't. She tossed the bloodied fabric at him. "Then you do it."

He snatched the dishtowel out of the air before the rag could hit him in the face.

"I didn't mean…."

Yes, she was annoyed. She had no idea why, but it was fine. She didn't need to be acting out of character here.

She was just out of sorts with Marsh gone. She didn't like how the loss of her safety net made her vulnerable. And annoyed as hell—she'd just given away a crucial piece of information. No one rattled her. But within the span of a few minutes Hamish Ballard had gotten her to reveal that she knew Beatrice's skill set. Dammit. Hopefully he had missed her flub. But she didn't have faith that he was that unobservant.

She inhaled harshly.

His gaze dipped to her chest. Lingered.

That was one way to distract him from his line of questioning.

But that move backfired on her as Jill's body reacted without her permission. Again. Her nipples tightened, probably visible beneath her cream silk blouse. She pressed her lips together. This attraction was inconvenient.

"Sure doesn't feel like anyone has been here in a while." The apartment had a musty, unoccupied air.

"I told you he's on sabbatical," she gritted out.

He let go of her wrist and she breathed a sigh of relief.

He rubbed his hands together like an old-fashioned villain. "Could he be working with a…client?"

"None of your business."

"Maybe he took on Brianna Walsh on the side." He was trying to give her an out. A way to pretend that she didn't know anything about Beatrice.

But she didn't jump at the opportunity. "No. We are equal partners. We don't take on clients without a major consultation and agreement from our staff. Some public relations problems don't fit our model and we refer them if we can't help."

"So then what were you doing here? Looking for files?" Hamish prodded.

"We don't take any information out of our office. Our files are secure," she growled. Ugh. He wasn't going to give up. And she needed to formulate a plan to deal with Hamish Ballard. Normally she'd come up with something on the fly, but nothing was normal about today and she needed to regroup and attack this again tomorrow.

"Let's meet in the morning at ten." She needed to get away from him. Think. Plan. Come up with a way to find Beatrice and maybe Marsh? Before the blowhard.

And tomorrow at ten, she'd be conveniently out of the office to meet with Dee. She'd have Kita take the meeting and stall him.

In the past few minutes, they'd somehow drifted closer to each other, like metal shavings to a magnet. All the little pieces of her gravitated toward him.

Jill shoved out her hand to create some distance between them. "Truce?"

When he took it, that jolt didn't surprise her quite so much. She managed to portray cool and collected.

He stared at her as if he knew she had no intention of working with him. "Sure."

A wave of exhaustion rolled over his face. He suddenly looked bone-deep tired. She could literally see him sway on his feet. "You okay?"

"Aye." He rubbed his blunt-tipped fingers over his face and blinked hard. "Been awake for a few hours over the day mark. Need a little sleep."

"Tomorrow then?"

He hesitated. "Aye."

That soft brogue rolled through her like a lover in the dark, tempting her with things she couldn't have and had no business wanting. She had all night to get her hormones under control.

Still it was a good thing she'd be out tomorrow when he came calling.

Chapter 5

Jillian Larsen was a fraud.

She'd thrown out that ten a.m. meeting time knowing full well she already had an appointment scheduled across town. And Hamish had no intention of letting her get the jump on him this morning. He'd done recon on the ALIAS building and grounds and identified that her most likely entrance to the building was the small parking lot in the back whether she drove or took a taxi to the office. He'd gotten takeaway, an Americano for her and a cuppa for him, and sat on the brick stoop leading to the back door of the building.

He had spent the night listening to the transmission from the bug for any movement in her office in case she went back without him. Okay, and maybe dozing because he was tired AF.

At half six in the morning a sleek, sparkling, pearl-white Tesla zipped into the small lot. The frigid morning air nipped at his skin. Steam rose from the paper cups and the hot liquids warmed his palms. She swung out of her car and strode confidently toward the door.

Hamish knew the exact moment she saw him. The slight hitch in her stride and the pinch of her red glossy lips gave away her surprise and annoyance.

She wore a trim wool peacoat in a red that matched her lips, shiny black patent pumps, and a tight skirt that cupped her spectacular arse and ended just below her knees revealing slender muscular calves. Her blond hair was pulled tight into an austere knot at the base of her skull. The severe style showcased her sharp cheekbones and highlighted her classic beauty. He mentally cursed his body as his cock thickened.

She was totally peng. Buttoned up and serious but gorgeous. A glamorous executive with a quick intellect and nothing like what he had expected. She hadn't hesitated to defend herself last night. And he would admit that he'd lain awake reliving the moments when she'd cleaned the cut on his forehead, her soft breath on his face and the lush curves of her breasts at his eye level.

His body hadn't gotten the message that she was off limits, and his brain needed to get on board. In many ways she was similar to Brianna Walsh, who wore glamour like a shield with a bombshell body and generous womanly curves. But Brianna's beauty hid an evil soul.

He wasn't sure what Jillian's mask guarded but he would love to find out. If only he had the time.

"Good morning." He smiled broadly.

Her lips tightened in a parody of a smile. Even this early she was perfectly together, but pale beneath the flawless makeup. She appeared to have gotten as much sleep as he had.

"You're up early," she said.

"Eager to get a jump on the day."

She raised an eyebrow.

So he lied. "Time difference. Been up for hours." That was the truth. And his thoughts hadn't all been about Brianna.

She jangled her keys in her hand.

Ten o'clock, my arse.

He had been correct to arrive early. Hamish was ready to convince her to share her information about Brianna. He wasn't going to be left behind. This fake truce she'd proposed last night was just that. Fake.

And he had no intention of giving up.

Last night he'd gone over his files on Brianna. Then he'd dug into Jillian Larsen's past again, reviewing his information about her final job and departure from the US Marshals. There was more to that story than what had been released. Why had no charges been filed against her? Ostensibly she was no longer working in the law enforcement community. Except she still had ties. That was clear.

However, being antagonistic wasn't going to get him very far. So he'd decided to attempt to use his charm. "I brought you a coffee."

She blinked. That had thrown her. "Thank you."

She opened the door, multiple locks and a beeping alarm system. She angled her body and punched in an eight-digit code.

Hamish discreetly slipped his hand in his pocket and pressed the record button on his mobile. He would record the telltale sounds and try to recreate the sequence just in case. But when she placed her palm on a reader that slid out after the coded entry, he realized he was going to be out of luck.

Jill reached for the paper cup, and he held the carrier tightly so she could tug it out.

"I've got cream and sweetener."

"Not necessary." She blew on the hot liquid with pursed lips. He tried and failed to ignore her sexy red mouth. Then she tilted her head back, exposing the long slender curve of her neck as she closed her eyes and apparently had a religious experience with her morning beverage. The soft hum could be mistaken for many things including arousal. And dammit, his body reacted to her erotic moan.

What he'd like was to hear that sound while he was tasting *her*.

He cleared his throat.

"Needed that." She sighed and her eyes drifted open, revealing a blurry dove gray. The sharp, take-no-prisoners business owner, protecting her partner and her contacts, had disappeared and in her place was a soft, pliable woman with a capital W. Up close he could see the faint blue shadows beneath her eyes and the fatigue that wasn't quite disguised by her perfect makeup.

He wanted to soothe, to protect. Which okay sure that was usually his MO but not now and not with this woman. She had information that would help him find Brianna. And she was hiding it from him.

He couldn't afford to feel sympathy for her. He needed the reminder that she was not his friend, nor would she be his lover.

"Let's get started, shall we?"

She stiffened, the softness burning away. She led the way to her office, turning on the building's lights as she went. The office was in an old brownstone, converted from a single family home into a comfortable and expensive work space.

He paid more attention this time as he followed behind her, taking in the Persian carpet, the reinforced steel doors, an open gym with free weights and pads and benches for serious weight lifting.

"You lift?"

"Everyone does daily PT." Jill tacked on, "Including self-defense."

He raised a brow and skimmed his gaze over her body. "Nice."

He let the suggestive tone linger. He was drawn to her. He was pretty sure she was attracted too, and clearly she wasn't opposed to getting involved with subjects in an active op, based on her history. Maybe that was the way to play this. Indicate his interest and see if she took the bait.

Hamish shoved away the feelings of guilt. He was going to use her. The means justified the end result if he could find Brianna and bring her to justice.

She shoved open the door to her office and then let it swing shut, the thick wood slab practically banging him in the face.

The door hit him with a thud. "Oof."

"Not going to work." She tossed over her shoulder as she carefully placed her sleek leather bag on the credenza behind her massive desk. "But nice try. The accent is…persuasive."

Hamish gritted his teeth. Good to know she was immune. The acute sense of disappointment took him by surprise. And he'd admit, if only to himself, that perhaps the idea hadn't been all ploy. But she'd never believe him.

"Well then, let's get down to it."

"Let's."

The door burst open. "Remind me never to drink with a Russian again!"

A petite Asian woman with a waterfall of long black hair barreled into the office, wearing spandex leggings and a loose tank top that bared her shoulders and ripped arms, and carrying a laptop like a football. "What the hell did you —" She stopped abruptly when she saw Hamish.

"Oh." She began to back out of the room. "Sorry to interrupt."

"Come on in, Kita." Jill waved the woman in.

She continued to stare at Hamish with a suspicious gaze. And Jillian did nothing to dispel her blatant suspicion.

So Hamish stood. "Hamish Ballard." He thrust out his hand.

"Kita Kim. My resident computer guru." Jill introduced the woman.

Hamish blinked and likely did a piss poor job of hiding his surprise. Why had Jillian requested an early morning meeting with her computer specialist?

Jill smirked.

He shoved away his confusion and held out his hand. "How do you do."

"Hamish is in town for information on a PR client."

He barely held back a jolt. Yesterday she had denied even knowing Brianna. What was she up to?

"Is that so?" Kita plopped into on the crewel-embroidered wing chair. "And you think we can help you?"

"I hope so." He turned on the charm, but he knew right away that this Kita would be immune. "Your agency worked with Beatrice Winter."

"The America's Recovery Centers case?" Kita didn't move but she stiffened slightly. She glanced at Jillian as if waiting for permission. Hamish almost missed Jillian's imperceptible nod. Kita rubbed at a bruise on her jaw. "We did some PR work, social media seeding for her, sure. But that was a few months ago."

Hamish eyed Jillian. This was the first time that anyone

had admitted that they had contact with Brianna. He raised his brows at her. *So now you admit she's a client?*

She shrugged. "We protect our clients."

He glanced between the two of them. "Were you aware that Beatrice Winter has disappeared?"

Her tension was subtle, and Jillian Larsen was giving her office mate a solid, inscrutable look.

Kita laughed. "Unlikely."

"Why do you say that?"

"Because no one truly disappears. They just mask their location."

"Can you figure out where she is?"

"I'm assuming that if you can't find her, she doesn't want to be found." Kita didn't budge.

"Perhaps, but I need to speak with her."

"Why?"

"She is wanted in the UK."

"Doubtful," Kita shot back.

This was getting annoying. "Why are you so sure?"

"The press would have glommed on to that tidbit if it were true. Journalists are vultures."

"Unless the British government gave her perfect papers."

Which fuck him, they had. She'd manipulated the authorities, the jury, and the judge into believing that she'd been forced to work in the family "business." They'd believed her sob story after she'd testified against her mob family, even though she had been complicit in many of the illegal activities that her family had been convicted of.

Her sweet face and soft innocent façade had fooled everyone.

She was pure evil.

He clenched his hands into tight fists. They'd all been

taken in by her appearance. Her charming sorrow and her insincere apologies for the sins of her family had been soaked up by everyone. Including him.

She'd managed to betray her family and get a new start in the US. And she might have gotten away with it if she'd stayed under the radar. Instead she had gotten involved in another criminal enterprise and screwed over her bosses yet again.

No one had been looking at Brianna for actually supplying drugs until Hamish learned she'd been his brother's pusher.

Unfortunately, the British government had been unwilling to track down Brianna Walsh now Beatrice Winter and charge her with drug dealing.

But since she'd moved to the US and committed crimes here, she'd broken her agreement with the British government. If he could find her, he could bring her in and make her face justice.

Hamish purposely kept relaxed. But it was hard.

Jillian eyed him speculatively. "She didn't have an accent," Jill said suddenly. "You sure this is the same woman?"

"She's a very accomplished actress," Hamish gritted out. She fooled everyone.

Jillian stepped toward him, her shoulders tense. "Still not a crime."

"She's a criminal." Hamish wanted to snarl and snap, but he kept his voice even. His mouth was set in a grim line. He took another step toward her as if he could convince her with his sheer bulk.

"You still haven't told me what she did?"

He knew that if he told them about his brother's

journal, they wouldn't help. He needed to start with well-documented facts and hope he could sway them with those.

"She comes from an Irish mob family. About two years ago, she testified against them in a rather large trial."

"Name?" Kita barked.

"Brianna Walsh."

Kita began banging on her laptop keys.

"That doesn't make her relocation to the states illegal. She just wanted out from under her family's oppression," Jill argued, taking another step toward him.

Kita glanced from Hamish and to Jill, clearly picking up on the tension between the two.

"We all know that families can be difficult." Jill crossed her arms, drawing his gaze to the modest vee in her blouse. Just the shadow of cleavage stirred something dark and needy within him.

Hamish jerked his gaze back to her face. "No one is disputing that fact."

She had caught him looking at her breasts. He flushed. He wasn't about to back down, in fact he took another step closer.

"Having a shady family isn't a crime." Jill narrowed her eyes. Her gray gaze darkened to the color of the stormy sky.

"True. But basically she burned her family in the UK, got a new identity, moved to the US, and did the same thing all over again."

"What did she have to gain by testifying against the drug rehab centers?" Jill said.

"They never recovered the money," Hamish snarled, his temper finally getting the best of him.

"You said that last night but there was nothing in her background that suggested she stole money."

"And how would you be knowing that if all you did was PR and social media for her?" Hamish snapped back.

Jill blinked, and he could see that moment where she wanted to shift her gaze away, instead she held his defiantly. "You're right. We don't know anything about her finances or her skills."

He could tell the admission cost her.

"Last night?" Kita broke in.

They ignored her.

How many times did he need to repeat this? "She was the accountant, the money woman for her family. She knows how to conceal money, how to launder money and how to get away with it."

"She worked in marketing for the America's Recovery Centers."

"But she had an affair with the Finance Director." Hamish fisted his hands. "I'm guessing she had sex with him to gain access to the accounting system where she siphoned off funds."

With each point, he'd walked closer to her until they were mere inches apart. Heat rose between them.

The air vibrated with tension and a hint of sexual arousal.

"And then she tipped off the authorities that the centers were a scam." Jill tilted her head as if examining the idea for flaws.

Finally, he was making some headway.

"Um, this is all very compelling, but what makes you think she has disappeared?" Kita's question broke the strange tension between the two of them.

Hamish looked away from the magnetic force field of Jillian Larsen.

He refused to step back as if ceding ground was the

same as giving up. Jillian clearly felt the same way as she continued to stand too close to him.

"Her last known address was Florida, and the last contact was here in DC. With Adams-Larsen." Hamish clenched his fists and stared accusingly at Jill. "Why is that?"

"I have no idea." Jillian shook her head as if releasing from a trance and finally she stepped away from him. "Even if she was part of a crime family in the UK, she came to the US legally. So why is the National Crime Agency suddenly after her?"

Hamish's heart banged against his ribcage. If they called his boss, he'd be busted. "New information has come to light."

"What kind of information?"

"I am not at liberty to discuss it," Hamish said.

Jill rolled her eyes. "So all we have is your word, Officer Ballard?"

Hamish stiffened. "My word is golden." He'd built a reputation for being a solid investigator with temperament like a bulldog. He didn't let go until he cornered his prey and brought them down. That was how he approached problems, by banging away at them. And it had always worked. Until this year.

"Well, I'm sorry, but that isn't good enough for me," Jill said. "And you have no proof of your accusations. If you really want to clear this up, you need to speak with Beatrice."

"I've been trying to find her for months. She is missing. And I think Adams-Larsen knows where she is."

"Even if we did do some PR work for her, we don't divulge our client's personal details," Jillian said.

"If you have any information regarding her whereabouts, you need to tell me."

"I'll have Kita look into it." Jill smiled tightly. It was a clear dismissal.

"Every minute that you stall me is another minute where Brianna Walsh aka Beatrice Winter gets away with murder."

"Murder?" Jill jerked back. "What are you talking about?"

Hamish shook his head. "Nothing," he muttered.

"Are you saying she killed someone?" Jill persisted.

"She duped everyone," Hamish said.

"While this may be true, it has nothing to do with Adams-Larsen. Unless you have proof she murdered someone." Jill frowned. "Then we can alert the authorities."

Hamish couldn't say more without giving himself away. He needed to find Brianna yesterday.

"Give me a few hours to look into these new accusations." She dismissed him. "I'll give you a call later."

Since Hamish knew she had an appointment in a little while, he let her dismissal slide. He planned to follow her to Deanna Womack's office and to see if she went anywhere else. He could listen in on her conversations in this office. He'd probably learn more that way as it was since she wasn't about to admit to a thing.

But he wasn't giving up. Ever.

____

Chapter 6

____

J ill pulled into a guest spot at the US Marshal's office in Arlington, Virginia and turned off her car.

The *tick tick tick* of the engine settled in her chest as she centered herself and got ready for this meeting. It seemed inconceivable that Dee had known that Beatrice was actually from the UK. She had told Marsh and Jill that her office had a leak regarding a witness. And after looking at Beatrice's case, they had agreed to relocate her. But now Jill had to wonder if there was more behind Dee's request.

Jill smoothed her hand over her pencil skirt and checked the rearview mirror for any flaws in her makeup. Going back into her old office was always unsettling. Even though it had been years since she left, there were still people around who remembered her. Despised her. Hated her might even be a more accurate depiction.

Most days, that didn't bother her at all. But for some reason this morning, her heart tattooed a funky beat in her chest.

Jill took a deep breath and exited her car. She strode confidently to the entrance and opened the door without hesitation. The motto etched into the glass—Justice. Integrity. Service—reminded her of all the things she'd publicly rejected in order to save her lover.

Her gait was unconcerned and casual as she approached the security desk.

"Jillian Larsen here to see Deanna Womack." She smiled at the guard, a kid who barely looked out of high school, and waited him for him to call up to Dee's office.

Within a few minutes, Dee's new administrative assistant clicked and clacked her way to the security desk. "Ms. Larsen, come this way."

Based on the glacial attitude of the young woman, Jill's reputation had preceded her. She gave the infant girl, who looked as if she'd never made a difficult choice in her life, a cool smile and strode in front of her toward the elevator. Jill punched the number for the proper floor, silent as the elevator doors slid closed.

The impersonal building crammed full of government workers made her grateful for the welcoming and intimate work environment of Adams-Larsen. The elevator doors opened to the smell of stale coffee, ink from the copy machines, and the faint underlay of gun oil. The ringing of telephones, rustle of papers, and the chatter of multiple conversations in the large open space assaulted her ears.

The murmurs and clacking of computer keys faded as a hush fell over the office floor.

"Jill, how…good to see you." Bob Miller, her partner on Dominic's case, was still bitter that she'd rejected him. He'd never gotten over the fact that she'd chosen Dominic over him. She was pretty sure he'd toasted her dismissal with a growler of Atlas IPA.

"Hey!" Alex Saunders, Kita's new boyfriend, who she had moved in with after two weeks of dating, came up to Jill and grabbed her by the elbows. He leaned in for a quick hug and then stepped back. They had bonded over a tense situation last month when Kita had been kidnapped, and Jill and Alex had to come up with a plan to save her. Except Kita had managed to save herself.

"Good to see you, Alex." With Alex's gesture, the office resumed its normal hustle and bustle. Conversations quickly regained their prior volume. People were still watching, they were just being more discreet about it.

"If you'll come this way," Dee's admin said snippily.

Jill had been freezing out judgy people like this girl for years.

"See you later, Alex." She winked at him.

After running the gauntlet between the elevators and Dee's office, her stomach twisted although she should would sure as hell never show any discomfort to these people. She had perfected the carefree, nonchalant attitude years ago, and the minor annoyance of judgmental former coworkers couldn't rattle her.

Everyone had been quick to believe that she was so unprofessional that she was lax about security because she was having an affair with her witness and let him get killed. Then she had the temerity to leave without censure and start her own successful business. She understood why people hated her. What she didn't understand was how many people she worked with, people she had considered friends, were quick to believe her so negligent.

That had been eye-opening.

None had cut so deep as the contempt of her father.

What no one seemed to understand was that Jill had loved Dominic. Or at least she thought she had. But she had let him go to save his life.

"Jill." Dee smiled and came around her desk to shake Jill's hand.

Dee's grip was tight, tough. In her mid-fifties, she was an original badass who had worked her way up to a supervisory position. Jill had always admired her for forging the path in what used to be primarily a man's profession. At one time, Dee had been her mentor. As such, Jill had studied her relentlessly, wanting to emulate her.

"That will be all, Leticia. If you would close the door on your way out."

Jill sat in the uncomfortable chair across from Dee's desk and waited for her former boss to speak.

After the door thumped closed, Dee said, "So why did you want to see me?"

Jill hesitated. Did she really want to reveal Hamish's name and his story? It might be prudent to hold that in reserve. "There's this guy."

"You really want to put your trust in some guy?" Dee said. "Didn't you learn your lesson last time?"

Ouch. That hurt. Her affair with Dominic and falling in love with him had not been the smartest move, but he had never betrayed her trust. And the cynical derision in Dee's voice was new.

"Strike that. I have a few questions about Beatrice Winter and I was wondering if you could answer them."

Dee's brows crimped. "I thought that was a done deal." Her gaze shot to the closed door and then she seemed to relax.

"Yeah, her relo is closed. I just was wondering if there was any new information on the money."

"The money? What does that have to do with Bea?" Before Jill could answer, Dee said, "The executives are still insisting they don't have the money and never did."

"But no one has found it." Jill tapped her index finger on her lips. "Is it possible that Beatrice took the money?"

Dee started. "I certainly hope not." But there was something there. A small warble in Dee's voice so slight that if Jill hadn't explicitly been listening, she wouldn't have heard it. She studied her old mentor. Dee's impassive face was hiding something, piquing Jill's curiosity even further.

"How did you vet her before sending her to us?" Because maybe she and Marsh hadn't asked the correct questions when Dee had come to them. The truth was they had owed her for finagling Jill's dismissal and Dee had played on that outstanding debt. She had also over the years sent some clients their way if they didn't meet the parameters needed to qualify for WitSec.

Dee's eyes narrowed. "Same as always."

"Is there any chance that Beatrice wasn't a US citizen?"

"Of course she was."

But Jill wasn't so sure. Hamish Ballard might be her adversary because he threatened to expose Adams-Larsen, but he believed what he'd been saying about Beatrice. And because of that unshakable belief, Jill needed to know that Dee hadn't sold them out.

Jill had had some reservations about Beatrice, but she'd pushed them aside because Dee had asked, and Marsh had been handling it.

"Where are you getting these crazy ideas?" Dee frowned at her as if concerned by her mental state. "She was a marketing specialist."

"Just something that came across my desk." No way was she going to share that the something was a five-foot-ten hunk with a Scottish accent and a serious case of hard-on for their client. "And it had me wondering."

"What does Marsh have to say?"

Marsh? Why was Dee asking about Marsh? As if Jill didn't have the credentials to be investigating.

Maybe Dee had begun to buy into the fictional story that they'd put out saying that Marsh had been the one who rescued Jillian from herself. The truth was they had rescued each other.

"Marsh was a little too close to our subject." Jill remembered the electric tension the moment Beatrice walked into ALIAS's Georgetown office. Marsh had been enthralled with their client, absolutely smitten by her.

"We rushed her relo through pretty quickly," Jill said. "And now, little details are nagging at me."

"So where is she?"

Jill couldn't believe Dee had asked. "You know I can't tell you that."

"Is she somehow making trouble for you?" Dee asked.

"Nope. Not at all."

There was a slight sheen of sweat on Dee's forehead. But it was cool sixty-five degrees in this office. She tended to run hot and always kept it quite chilly. The sweat could just be because she was warm. But Jill didn't think so. Was Dee hiding something?

"That's good to hear."

Jill said, "I just wanted to make sure that everything is clean and clear with her case."

Dee laughed, the sound a slightly nervous chuckle. And Jill knew that something was totally off. "You would know better than me. I turned over all her files to you."

Files Jill could no longer find. Shit. "Okay, well if anything relating to her case comes up, can you loop me in? I just want to make sure that we didn't overlook something that could come back and bite ALIAS in the ass."

"Will do." Dee's relief seemed out of proportion.

"How's everything?" Jill asked.

"Pretty good." Dee relaxed. "I'm up for a promotion, assuming nothing goes sideways with my current caseload."

"Excellent news." Jill was happy for her mentor. "When will you find out?"

"Next few months." Dee shrugged. "Unfortunately it's cost me my relationship. But that's the breaks."

"I'm sorry to hear that." Jill had always been envious of the fact that Dee and her wife had seemed to be solid.

"Yeah well, relationships in this business are hard." Dee stared into the distance. "Our demise was inevitable."

That was a seriously depressing thought.

Dee believed they were destined to be alone.

Sure Jill didn't date much. And sure, she always thought that she'd settle down…one day. But she'd never met *the one.*

Viktor had thought his boyfriend was the one. He'd been certain. And he'd been wrong. That was closer to what Jill expected with relationships.

But her pal, Bliss Lee, had met her *one* years ago.

Jill had thought Bliss had been exaggerating when she tried to explain her connection to Jack Stone. But when Bliss was forced to work with her old flame on a case, the attraction had flared back to life and she was happily married now.

Jill would admit that she held Bliss and Jack Stone up as the model for a healthy relationship. She wanted that…someday.

Except, with Marsh gone these past few months, she had realized how empty her life was. And suddenly that emptiness chafed.

She refused to believe that some sort of happy compromise wasn't possible.

Dee seemed fatalistic that her relationship with her wife had been destined to fail.

But as Jill left, she wondered. She had always admired Dee. But there'd been something in her attitude that grated on Jill.

Jill replayed the conversation with Dee as she drove back to the office. Her thoughts were distracted and bouncing around. She'd had the uncomfortable feeling of being watched on her way to Dee's office. And now, she noticed that she might have a tail.

So she began a standard SDR, surveillance detection route, to see if someone was following her. Within a few minutes she realized that she was indeed being followed. And the jerk in her rearview was none other than Hamish Ballard.

She steamed on the ride back to her office, forgoing additional evasive maneuvers since she knew who it was.

What the hell was he doing?

HAMISH KNEW that she saw him. He hadn't tried to hide on the way home.

She'd gone to her former employer's location and met with her former boss, causing a lot of questions to churn through his brain. Because if she'd left in disgrace, why would she be meeting with her former agency? And she set up the meeting right after he visited her office yesterday.

Hamish pulled into the ALIAS parking lot like he worked there and took one of the remaining two spaces. He hopped out of his rental car as Jillian slammed her car door and glared at him with her fist propped on her hip and an unholy light in her fiery eyes. "You followed me."

He shrugged. "I wanted to know where you were going. I didn't make any effort to hide."

Her gaze narrowed and she studied him. "We're done." She pivoted quickly and strode toward the back entrance to the brownstone. Her heels clicked in an aggravated beat on the blacktop.

"I have something to show you."

She held up her hand in the universal gesture for "I don't give a fuck" and didn't look back. He'd been hoping to avoid sharing this since technically he did not have approval to show the file to anyone, but every moment ticked toward his inevitable return to Edinburgh. And so far he had nothing to show for this trip. Hamish strode after her and hoped he was making the right decision. "You want to see this."

"Not interested." She shoved her key into the old-fashioned lock and turned. Then she jabbed the buttons to enter the eight-digit code and waited for the biometric reader to appear. The door clicked open and before she could slam it in his face, he inserted his shoulder, stopping her. The move put them closer together than socially appropriate, his chest nearly touching her back. This close he could feel the fury that vibrated through her body. The sultry scent wafting from her hair was sensuous and earthy, a contradiction to her buttoned-up attitude.

They were trapped in a small holding area, with another solid wood door blocking entrance to the building. An additional keypad and more biometric security in the wall to the left of the second doorknob closely guarded the entrance.

A disembodied voice came out of nowhere. "Jill, do you need assistance?"

Hamish skimmed his gaze over the small vestibule,

looking for a speaker. Then he glanced up and saw the camera in the corner. Earlier today he had noted the multiple checkpoints before anyone could actually enter the building. Each small holding area had additional security with either biometric scanners or passcodes necessary. The dark mahogany wainscoting and glass door at the exterior appeared decorative but he'd bet his credentials that the glass was bulletproof and the door frame construction reinforced. It wouldn't necessarily keep someone out indefinitely, but the inhabitants would have plenty of notice before a combatant breached the interior. Those security measures only increased his surety that Adams-Larsen was no public relations firm.

However, it was much easier to come in the front door as he had. That solid construction didn't have any windows.

"You need to understand what kind of person she really is." Hamish shoved a file folder filled with papers at her.

She backed up and pressed against the door frame. "What is this?"

"This is the transcript from Brianna Walsh's deposition. Much of this didn't make it in the trial because the prosecution wanted a credible witness and the defense negotiated its omission from the sentencing phase to limit the jury's knowledge of her complicity." Hamish wanted to shake the file in her face.

Slowly she curled her fingers around the only information he was willing to share at this point.

"Read it," he demanded. "And then give me a call."

He knew the power of a strategic retreat. If ever there was a time, this was it. He flipped a salute at the security camera in the ceiling, then directed a hard stare at Jillian Larsen—who hadn't said a word.

He slipped out into the cold morning air and headed

back to his place to eavesdrop on his infuriating, and distracting, nemesis. As he left, he tossed the parting words over his shoulder. "I'll wait to hear from you."

THE OUTER DOOR thunked closed behind Hamish Ballard. Jill's heart beat erratically in her chest as she faced away from the security camera and tried to regain her calm.

There'd been something in that fraught moment when he'd nearly pressed against her. His hard chest and thick biceps caged her, but she hadn't felt threatened. The truth was she trained regularly with Kita and while in a fight she might not win, she could hold her own and she could definitely kick his ass to the floor a few times. But in that moment, she hadn't been thinking about fighting, she'd been thinking about how long it had been since she'd been with anyone.

Her sex life was always…difficult. She couldn't tell her date what she really did, she couldn't share the details of her day, unless they were a lie, and that made it challenging to connect with another person. If you were only giving half of yourself, only revealing half of yourself, then how did a man ever understand who you were? The answer: He didn't.

"Jill, you okay?" Jake was in the security booth this morning.

"Fine. I'm fine." Jill hustled up the back stairs to her office, clutching the file folder in her hand.

She nodded at Maria and the new girl Hannah. "I'll be in my office if you need me for anything." She closed the door with a quiet snick and headed for her desk.

Jill dropped into the large ergonomic but elegant chair, flipped open the file, and began to read.

At first she denied the connection. The words could have come from anyone. But when she mentioned her family forcing her to get the tattoo, a sense of dread rolled through Jill. The Celtic knot with a stylized *W* entwined was distinctive.

She remembered when she'd first seen it.

In her office, Beatrice had been sitting on the settee and the hint of the tattoo had peeked out the hem of her shirtsleeve on her upper arm.

Marsh had been enthralled. Beatrice had seemed annoyed but then she'd quickly masked the annoyance and called it a youthful mistake.

In the transcript, she related the story of when her father had made her get the tattoo. She called it a brand. A mark that claimed she could never abandon her family.

As Jill read, her stomach churned like the Potomac on a stormy day. Beatrice Winter was not who they thought she'd was.

Daughter of a mobster in Ireland. Intricately involved in their illegal businesses. She had tearfully told the prosecution lawyers that she'd been forced to do the books and was basically an indentured servant her entire life. But reading between the lines, Jill didn't get that impression.

As she read the transcript, she noted that Brianna aka Beatrice was the one who had turned in evidence against her family. They would have had nothing without her testimony and records. Her father and two brothers, Category A offenders, were serving life sentences in Her Majesty's Prison Wakefield, the equivalent of a supermax in the US.

She had single-handedly taken down her family business after her mother passed away. According to the file, all of the family assets had been seized. But assets could be hidden. Even so, Jill need another pair of eyes on this.

Jill hesitated.

Protecting the client was her first priority. But what did she do if the client turned out to be a criminal?

And of course this was what Hamish Ballard had wanted. To make her doubt her convictions. To make her doubt her actions. She needed another opinion, an objective one.

Jill had no choice but to ask for help.

She pressed the intercom button on her phone set up. "Maria, can you send Kita up to my office?"

"Sure thing, Jill."

About five minutes later, Kita burst into Jill's office. "What do you need me for?"

She nodded at the open door, and Kita raised her brows as she quietly closed the door, leaving them alone and isolated in the quiet room.

"I came into the possession of the deposition transcripts and the trial summary from Beatrice Winter aka Brianna Walsh's trial." Jill was only about halfway through, but the more she read, the more she thought that Beatrice was a con artist of the highest order. She handed Kita the stack of papers she'd already read through and said, "I need you to read this, and give me your take on our former client."

Kita nodded and settled into the chair across from Jill's desk. She tucked her head down and focused. Jill continued to read the transcripts. With every page, her frustration grew.

Beatrice Winter's identification sources were perfect. Yes, she could have bought her passport and birth certificate. But the Marshals should have caught forged identity papers.

So did that mean that Beatrice had actually been

supplied with official documents that would stand up to scrutiny from the US authorities?

That was suspect. It was possible that Brianna Walsh was in the UK equivalent of WitSec. And it was more than a little suspicious that once again, she was the key witness for the prosecution in a criminal trial. How had her concealed background ever made it past the Department of Justice and US Marshals?

Her office was quiet as she and Kita continued to read through Hamish Ballard's comprehensive file. As she turned the last page, the headache brewing behind her eyes blossomed from a slight ache to a full on barrage. She rubbed her fingers at her temple, closing her eyes and wondering what the hell they had done.

Jill considered options as she waited for Kita to finish the file. They needed to find Beatrice Winter. And Marsh, if possible. Were they together? Jill certainly hoped not.

Kita finished leaned back in the chair and sighed.

"What's your take?"

Kita tossed the file onto Jill's desk. "I'm no psychologist, but the subtext in her testimony is clear. She hates men. She was continuously told by her father and brothers she wasn't good enough when it sure appears that she was actively running the business." They had pissed her off and she took them down.

"Yeah, that was my assessment as well." Shit. "So why did she target Marsh?" Because when she'd first come to ALIAS, Beatrice had requested that Marsh be her point man. And they'd grown close. So close, Jill was pretty sure that Marsh was having sex with her. But since Jill had no room to criticize, and they were making Beatrice disappear, she let it go.

"So she could manipulate him, I'd bet she really gets off

on pulling one over on men," Kita said.

"We have to talk to Beatrice. And find Marsh."

"But we've already tried to find him." Kita rubbed her palms over her bare biceps.

"Did you find anything interesting when you pulled Marsh's credit card records?" Jill asked.

"Yeah, after we placed Beatrice, Marsh left for the Cape for a few days."

That meshed with what Marsh said he was going to do. He had seemed a little…depressed after Beatrice was gone. Jill had told him to take as much time as he needed.

"And then what?"

"Then he went to Philadelphia."

Philadelphia. That's where they'd placed Beatrice.

Why the hell would Marsh jeopardize their client's safety by going to the one place he was expressly forbidden to visit? At least right away. "Fuck."

"Assuming that isn't good." Kita was somber.

Only Marsh and Jill knew they'd relocated Beatrice to Philly. Even now, she was struggling to reveal that simple detail to Kita. "What the hell was he thinking?"

"I got nothing." Kita shook her head. "Maybe he was enthralled with her Super Pussy."

Jill snorted. "What the hell, Kita? Super Pussy?"

"Marsh's kryptonite is damsels in distress. This chick played on that." Kita gestured to the file. "The transcript is littered with men she manipulated to do her bidding."

That was true.

"Looks like the Scottish Hottie was right. She's a criminal. And she…got away with it."

"Would you quit using that term?" Jill flushed.

Kita giggled. "What? The Scottish Hottie?"

She was just full of nicknames today. "What's gotten

into you?"

Kita laughed full on and then turned bright red. "I can tell what hasn't gotten into you."

What? Now they were girlfriends? Jill glared at Kita. But her face burned.

"Come on. Admit it's a little funny. You are attracted to him."

What now?

"The room was practically on fire from the sparks you two were emitting earlier." Kita fanned herself. "I had to go take a shower."

"There were no sparks."

"Keep telling yourself that."

"Guy is so uptight, he's probably a dud in bed."

"I don't care to find out, I've got my own personal hottie." Kita paused. "But if you have a chance, you should go for it."

Images of Hamish Ballard naked and moving over her flashed in her brain, but she banished them immediately. Okay maybe she had dreamed about him last night. But it was purely stimulus and response. He was the stimulus and she responded. She just hadn't gotten laid in a while.

"Can we get back on track here?" Jill snipped.

Kita eyed her warily. "Sure."

"I need to go to Philly," Jill said softly. "What hotel did Marsh stay at?" Presumably it was listed on his credit card records.

"The Sheraton downtown."

That's where Jill would stay.

"According to the bill he was only there a few days."

"Where did he go after that?"

"That's the last time he used the card." Kita leaned forward in her chair. "You want me to come with you?"

"I think you and Alex should take a trip to the Cape."

Understanding blossomed in Kita's gaze. "A weekend getaway sounds great."

Maybe Marsh would be there. Or maybe he'd still be in Philly…with their client?

Still Jill didn't want to assume that Marsh had broken the rules. While she wanted to find out what Marsh had been doing in Philly, she needed to check on Beatrice, to ask her some pointed questions. While she was at it, she could see if Marsh was still there. Though she intended to speak with Beatrice, she certainly had no intention of revealing to Hamish Ballard what ALIAS really did, and she couldn't tell him she was going to be in contact with Beatrice. He'd be pissed when he realized that she'd left town, but she had her priorities.

Her first responsibilities were to protect her clients, protect her business, and protect her employees.

Hamish Ballard was dead last on that list. Check that. He wasn't even on the list. Displeasure wriggled in her subconscious because he would see this move as a betrayal. But she didn't owe him a thing.

No regrets.

Someone knocked on her door.

"Come."

Maria wouldn't have let just anyone pass.

Viktor poked his head inside. "Am I interrupting?"

"We were done," Jill said.

"How you feeling today, Hot Stuff?" Kita teased.

Viktor flushed.

He had looked a little pale. "You okay?"

"Took your advice." Viktor smiled ruefully. "A little too much to heart."

Jill raised an eyebrow.

"Man, that dude can put them away." Kita punched Viktor on the arm as she left. "That's for the bruise on my chin."

"I said I was sorry," Viktor protested. But Kita was already out the door.

"You met someone?"

"I usually have a high tolerance but…this guy at the bar last night was, phew." He shook his head. "I may have overindulged."

"May have?" Jill teased, liking the fact that today he wasn't so sad. Her advice had worked. And she took that as a W.

What about the one though? Of course, she managed to keep that question to herself.

"I'm not ready for anything serious," he said as if he'd read her mind. "I'll take Mr. Right Now for the moment. Sorry. TMI."

The interaction was getting a little too personal so Jill said abruptly, "What have you got for me?"

"I was able to test the original information given by Beatrice Winter for phase one."

The first phase in any relocation was misinformation, muddying the personal information of the client. Changing their accounts so they were impossible to verify. A misspelled middle name. A slight shift in the birthday of record. Changing one number in a phone number, street number, or zip code. Little shifts that helped confuse a skip tracer looking for an individual.

"All of her accounts had been closed and all the information had been obscured. If I hadn't had the original contacts, she would be mostly disappeared from her life in Florida."

"Mostly?"

"I did find one email address that I didn't originally test. It could be part of phase two but since I didn't work on it, but I don't think it was."

Phase two was disinformation. Canceling the client's original accounts then deliberately setting up utility accounts, email addresses, and PO box dead drops, running credit checks by apartment complexes, making it look like the client had moved to another area. Using an existing credit card in new places to throw off anyone who might be trying to track the client.

"Where did we implement phase two?"

"We had charges in Texas, California, and another town in Florida on the opposite coast from her original address."

They had planted information and data in several states, all far away from Philadelphia where they finally settled Beatrice.

Her new name wasn't in the files. That was to protect her in case their systems were ever compromised.

"I'm still tracing the information on that email. It came up when I did an in-depth search of her name."

"Okay. Can you keep following up on that?"

"Sure." He rubbed his forehead.

"Headache?"

He nodded.

Jill rummaged through her desk and pulled out a bottle of Tylenol tablets. She dumped four into her palm and handed them to Viktor.

"*Spasibo.*"

"Let me know what you find."

"Sure thing, *boss.*"

Jill blinked, inordinately pleased with affection in the simple word. Maybe she was getting the hang of this maternal thing.

Chapter 7

The next day Hamish tailed Jill discreetly, not wanting her to see him until they were on the plane. He couldn't afford for her to leave if she spotted him first. So he lurked behind a post, listening impatiently as the plane boarded. Tension tightened his shoulders and cramped in his gut. He had listened in on her conversations yesterday, knowing she was headed to Philadelphia early this morning. He had thought about going ahead of her, then decided against it.

Because what if she had information that wasn't revealed while he was listening? His goal was to track her movements. And to do that he first had to get up close to her just long enough to plant a tracker on her person.

But last night had gone on for an eternity. He had limited time left and eating up another sixteen hours hadn't sat well with him. He had researched Philadelphia but with only a city and a hotel name, the intelligence wasn't much to go on.

Finally, it was last call for boarding. He hustled onto the plane and they closed the door behind him. *Brilliant.*

Jillian couldn't get off to avoid him even if she wanted to. He made his way down the aisle until he saw her. He'd even managed to snag a seat across the aisle from her. She was dressed in another fitted skirt, but this time she wore a more casual sweater and cardigan in a soft pale gray. The outfit suited her. And the softer sweater didn't diminish her cool ice-queen vibe.

Her eyes widened as she saw him. "What are you doing here?" she hissed.

Hamish smiled tightly as he smushed his bag under the seat. The overhead was full and he was going to be jammed into his little space. Fortunately, it wasn't a long flight. "Checking out the seat of you Yanks' rebellion."

He sat down, buckled in, and waited for her explosion.

But Jill shifted in her seat, put on earphones, and picked up a ball of bright blue yarn and circular knitting needles. She began angrily knitting, focusing on the project in her hands as if he didn't exist.

Hamish shrugged. Didn't matter to him if she spoke with him or not. What he really hoped was she would lead him straight to Brianna, and once and for all he could get justice for his brother.

He observed Jill while a small beanie cap slowly took shape in her hands. It looked to be for a child and she was not even checking the pattern so she'd clearly done this before. He could practically see her wheels turning as she tried to figure out how he'd found her. Pretty sure the bug in her office was a lost cause after this. The element of surprise was blown and she would be on guard in the future.

He had hoped he would get more information about Brianna's location before they took off. All he knew was that they had relocated her to the Philadelphia area. Why Adams-Larsen had done so was also a mystery. Although the why shouldn't matter, it tugged at his subconscious like a boy on his mum's dress when he wanted a treat.

Philadelphia was too big for him to just go and wander around without more specific data. Hamish tapped her on the shoulder, and she whipped her head around. She deliberately put down her knitting and took out an earphone. With an aggravated tilt, she cocked her head. "What?"

"So, where you headed?" He tried to soften his face, tried to smile, but the edge must've crept through his voice. Because she looked as if she wanted to stab him with her plastic needles.

"Not your business." She returned to her knitting. Before she did, he could see the questions burning in her ice-gray eyes, but she refused to give in to her curiosity.

"This would all go a wee bit faster if you just gave me the information I needed."

"Trust *you*?" She shook her head and went back to ignoring him.

Okay. Trusting him was a long shot, he'd give her that. The odd thing was, *he* wanted to trust *her*. Even though she was the enemy and she had helped Brianna disappear. He had gleaned that from her conversations with Kita Kim in the last two days. But she'd also jumped on trying to find Brianna as soon as she read through the transcripts from the trial. So she truly hadn't known how evil Brianna was. The urge to trust her snaked through him even though he knew it was a mistake.

"I wager you have more questions."

She turned her head again and pierced him with a deadly stare. "You bugged my office."

Not a question.

Hamish could lie but she'd know the truth eventually anyway. He shrugged again. "Aye."

"Illegal surveillance can't be used in a court of law."

"I don't want to make trouble for you," Hamish said. "And it will be worth it if I catch her."

"Your persistence is confusing." Jillian gave up the pretense of knitting and shoved the project into her bag along with the earphones. "You going to tell me why you're so obsessed with this woman?"

"She's a case."

"Bullshit." She tapped her finger over her pale pink lips. And not for the first time something hot and forbidden stirred inside him. Jillian Larsen was lush. Sexy. And he really needed to get his brain in gear and remember that she was hiding his enemy, which made her his enemy too. But all he could think about was pressing into her, taking her mouth and releasing all the pent-up fury inside him. That fury had morphed from rage to a dark, deep desire.

"This is personal for you," she said intuitively.

"Every case is personal."

She snorted. "So what do you expect to get from following me?"

"In a perfect world, you lead me to Brianna and justice will be served."

"Justice?" She shook her head, the spun-silk white-blond hair catching on her soft gray sweater. "That's a little vague for me."

"Don't you believe in justice?"

"I believe in following a moral code that protects the innocent."

"Justice is the foundation of criminal prosecution. It gives closure to the victims and punishment for the perpetrators."

"Sometimes the best outcome isn't about justice. It's about setting things right." She studied him for another minute. "Why'd you become a law enforcement officer?"

"I wanted to catch bad guys." Which was basically true. Keep the streets safe for everyone. Instead he'd failed the ones closest to him. Hamish shook off the dark cloud. Thinking about his failures right now wouldn't help him find Brianna.

The only way to set things right was for his brother's killer to be in prison…or dead.

"So where are we going first?" Hamish rubbed his hands together.

"We?" Jill snorted and Hamish couldn't help but think about that nervous little giggle from her office yesterday when her employee had called him the Scottish Hottie.

Of course she'd then replied that perhaps he had a stick up his arse. He wasn't uptight. Just driven. He'd certainly like to show her that he could be passionate. And based on her responses to Kita, she was attracted to him.

Hamish leaned back in his seat and smiled. "I think *we* could be very good together." It certainly wouldn't be a hardship and he was willing to do anything to find Brianna Walsh.

Her lips parted in surprise. "Are you really going to go there?"

"I'm open to the idea." Hamish cocked an eyebrow.

"Well, just shut that down right now. There is no we."

He acquiesced for now, but he'd seen that little spark of uncertainty and that infinitesimal moment where she considered it. Even if it was mostly against her better judgement.

"Okay, no we. I'll rephrase the question. Where are you going first?" And he'd be right behind her.

"None of your business."

"That's where you'd be wrong, love," Hamish said. "Everything to do with Brianna, er, your Beatrice Winter, is my business."

"What makes you think I'm going to Philadelphia to see her?"

"You're smarter than that." Hamish still kept his expression easy, light but inside he seethed. She hadn't actually mentioned Brianna by name in her office but Hamish knew from her conversation with Kita yesterday that was why she was on this plane.

Jill studied her perfect French manicure. "Why would you think that I know where she is?"

"Let's not play this game," Hamish said. "Let's work together to bring her to justice."

"Nope. I hardly think our endgame is the same."

Likely not. But he wasn't about to give up.

"You know, wool would be warmer than that cotton." He reached out to finger the cotton, subtly planting the tracker on it.

"What do you know about yarn?"

"I grew up on a sheep farm." He made the peace offering sincerely, wishing he felt guilty about tracking her. "I'd be happy to get you some wool."

"Wool isn't what I need." She dismissed him again. Somehow he thought she was actually saying, "*You* aren't what I need."

The overhead bell dinged indicating the short flight was almost over. The flight attendants bustled through the aisles and cut off their access to conversation. By the time the aisles were clear, she was back to ignoring him again.

The plane landed with a bump, ending their tense standoff.

HAMISH FOLLOWED HER. She ignored him.

Jill slung her Hermès bag over her shoulder and made a beeline for the exit of the plane.

He had fucking bugged her office. What pissed her off even more was that it took her so long to figure it out. Then the bastard had the nerve to follow her off the plane with a lazy saunter.

No way was she leading him to where Beatrice Winter lived now.

Thanks to Kita's computer skills they had recovered some information from Beatrice's original file. Jill had known her relocation city was Philly, and Kita had been able to retrieve both her employer and her home address.

Beatrice had been placed in an apartment in downtown Philadelphia near a SEPTA line and within walking distance to her job.

First on her agenda, Jill called the office. Jake was on emergency call this weekend. "Hey, Jake."

"Problem?" Straight. To the point. No words wasted. That was Jake Brown.

"I need you to sweep my office for bugs."

"Seriously?" he burst out. Then he corrected his response. "Sure thing, boss."

"I would bet there are more than one. So be extra cautious."

"What should I do with them?"

"Crush them under your shoe heel and pretend they are someone's balls."

"Uh, Jill?" She heard Jake swallow.

"Okay, sorry. Just flush them down the toilet." She

hesitated. "But take a picture of them so I can see what they look like."

"You got it."

That done, she hustled to the rental car counter to pick up her subcompact. Before she left the counter, she leaned over and said to the attractive black woman waiting on her, "If a guy…about yea high—" she lifted her hand to Hamish's height, "—asks about me…rather than tell him you can't give out information about customers, would you give him false information?"

"Honey, you got problems?" The woman cocked her head, her shiny curls jiggling.

"You could say that," she muttered.

"Don't worry. I got you." She handed Jill the folio with her contract and sent her outside to pick up her car.

Jill left the rental car lot, carefully checking behind her, but she didn't see Hamish anywhere. The tension that gripped her shoulders didn't lessen. He'd proven to be very resourceful and dogged at keeping tabs on her. Just because she couldn't see him didn't mean he wasn't around somewhere. Damn him.

Jill eased into traffic and headed for downtown Philadelphia. Once she exited the city near her target she took another SDR, making sure that he wasn't following. After fifteen minutes of driving in circles, confirming she didn't have a tail, she pulled into a parking lot across the street from Beatrice's new place of employment.

Jill pulled out her cell phone and punched in the number for the advertising agency where Beatrice was employed. She waited as the phone rang.

"Mercury Advertising," said a perky voice on the end of the line.

"Hello." Jill ran her finger over the steering wheel as her

breath caught. Contacting a client after they'd been placed was a serious breach in their protocol, even though she believed the inconsistencies in Beatrice's background were alarming. She was stuck between her faith in Marsh and the fact that he had completely gone off the grid. Hamish Ballard's accusations were concrete enough that she needed to do this. She asked for Beatrice using her new identity.

There was a short pause and then the receptionist said, "I'm sorry. She is no longer with us."

Shock zinged through Jill. "Are you sure?"

"I'm afraid so."

"Can I speak with your human resources manager?"

The receptionist said, "Hold, please."

The phone rang several times before the human resources manager picked up. "How can I help you?"

Jill said pleasantly, "Hi, this is Constitution Employment Agency. We sent you an administrative assistant a few months ago."

"Yes?"

"Can you tell me why she didn't work out?"

"I have no idea." There was clacking of the keyboard.

"How long was she employed there?" Jill asked.

"She only stayed about a week."

"I am…very sorry to hear that." Jill thought for a minute. "Did she, by any chance, leave a forwarding address?"

"No. She called in one morning and said she wasn't coming back." The manager hesitated for a moment. "She never even picked up her paycheck."

"How…odd. Thank you for your time." Jill hung up and pulled out the file with the scarce details she had on Beatrice's relocation.

Beatrice Winter had quit a week into her new job. Jill

skimmed her finger along the single sheet of printed paper until she came to Beatrice's address. Sighing, she put the car in gear and headed to the apartment listed. But a sinking feeling in her stomach rumbled through her. She wanted to believe that Beatrice had found a different job and was still living in the place they had secured for her.

However, if the woman they had relocated was as manipulative and cunning as that transcript indicated, Jill had a bad feeling that Beatrice was going to be long gone.

Jill quickly drove to Beatrice's apartment building. They had purposely set her up near her new job and near public transit so that she didn't need a car. Jill walked into the old-fashioned apartment building, her heels clicking on the vintage black-and-white tiles. A guard sat behind the burled wood console with a desktop screen on his left and an old-fashioned phone system on his right. "Can I help you?"

"I sure hope so." Jill smiled and got a picture of Beatrice from her file. "Can you tell me if this woman lives here?"

"Can I see some identification?"

Her heart quickened. Now she was getting somewhere.

"Certainly." She pulled a business card from her leather folio. A fake business card. "She has recently come into an inheritance. And I simply need for her to sign in order for her to collect it."

The guard was still eyeing her suspiciously. "I'm sorry, she doesn't live here anymore."

"Are you sure?"

"Nobody gonna forget a lady like that," he said with a smile on his wide brown face.

"How long did she live here?"

"'Bout a week."

ALIAS had paid for her first three months upfront. "Any idea where she might have moved to?"

"You're going to have to talk to the manager about that."

"Is he or she here?"

"Let me see." He punched in some numbers on the phone system and waited as it rang. "Hey, Leonard. There's a lady here about the lady tenant who only stayed a week."

He listened for a moment then said, "Okay, I'll send her on up."

"Keep the card and if you see her, please give me a call. I'm sure she'd be willing to share some of that inheritance if you help her get it." Jill dangled the possibility of money with little subtlety.

"I surely will do that." He buzzed her through the next set of doors and Jill climbed a grand staircase to the second floor. Number 205 was already open and an ancient little man stood in the doorway.

"May I help you?" He had a wizened face and calculating eyes. He might be more inclined to help her.

"I hope so." Jill pulled out another business card. The fake business cards had the name of a fake law firm, Adam's Law Office, and a phone number that routed to ALIAS when needed. They used them when pretexting, fudging the truth, in order to get information. Technically, it wasn't exactly legal. But in this case Jill felt she didn't have a choice.

"What's this all about?"

Jill handed him her card. "She has come into an inheritance, and this is the last known location I have for her. I was wondering if she left a forwarding address?"

Jill forced herself into stillness, knowing that fidgeting would give her away. But the anxiety growing within her made it difficult. Beatrice Winter had disappeared.

"I'm sorry, but she didn't leave any address." He rubbed his leathery hands together. "As a matter of fact, she didn't even request her security deposit back. She was supposed to call me with her new address so I could send it, but she never did."

This was not good. "What about her furniture? Did she use a moving company?"

"No, ma'am." A frown perplexed his brow. "She left everything in her apartment."

"Everything?"

"Yes." Leonard shook his head. "It done looks like she just went to the store and never came back."

"Do you suspect foul play?" Jill's brain pinged in a different direction. Maybe someone had hurt Beatrice.

"No. She told me herself that she was leaving. And she didn't seem stressed or under duress, she just seemed to be in a hurry."

"Did she leave a phone number?"

"Yes she did." The old man shuffled to an old rolltop desk and pulled out a spiral-bound paper calendar with pictures of hotels in the Poconos. He flipped back to September and ran his finger along the notes section until he found it. "Here you go."

It was the cell phone Adams-Larsen had given her, so that was likely a dead end. But Jill noted the phone number down dutifully in her small book. "Thank you for your help."

"Happy to." Leonard tilted his head and looked at her card again. "Say…are you affiliated with the gentleman who came the week after she left?"

Jillian stilled. She knew she had to play this carefully. Was the gentleman Marsh? Or was it someone else?

"Was his name Marsh?"

He nodded.

Fuck.

"Why yes, I am," Jill said. "He was involved in the initial track down of our client's beneficiaries."

Maybe she could get some usable information from this manager. "Do you recall the date he was here?" Jill tapped through her phone as if looking for the information. "When he couldn't locate her, I was sent in, but there were some details missing from the file."

"Here it is." The man squinted at his paper notes. "He came the day after she left."

"Excellent. I will update our files. Thank you for that information." Jill's brain was racing. So Marsh had been looking for Beatrice when he went on his walkabout. But why? And what did he intend to do if he found her? Did he find her? And were they still together now? And why the hell hadn't he confided in Jillian?

"Is there anything else I can do for you?"

"If she shows up again, can you give me a call? Or if she calls you, can you give me a call?"

"Be happy to."

Jill's shoved out her hand and clasped manager's hand in hers.

"Since her lease is almost up, I was just about to rent the apartment out to a new tenant and I've been fretting about what to do with her things." His gaze was rueful. "I hate to sell her stuff but I can't afford to store it and I don't have the space to store it here once the new tenant moves in."

"You still have her belongings?"

"I sure do," the manager said. "I don't suppose you know anyone who might want them?"

Jill's thoughts jumbled. She would love to go through the apartment. "The estate would be willing to pick up the furniture and store it for her until we can find her."

"You sure?" The old man blinked, his rheumy eyes watering in surprise. "It's an expensive proposition."

"She's going to be a very wealthy woman. It's the least the estate can do." Not to mention, the furnishings had been purchased by ALIAS or, really, the federal government.

"That would be wonderful." The manager appeared to relax as if she had taken a great burden from him. "Thank you very kindly. I really hated the thought of just selling her furniture out from under her."

"Can I see the apartment?" Jill wanted a look at Beatrice's stuff.

He took out a set of keys and shuffled out of his apartment. "Technically, I shouldn't let you in there. But since you're willing to take care of emptying out the apartment, it's the least I can do."

Jill said, "I'll make some calls, and I should be able to get movers here to clear out the apartment by tomorrow."

He relaxed even further. "Excellent. Then I could get new tenants in by the first." The manager jingled his keys. "Come on and I'll let you in the apartment."

Jill's hope buoyed. Maybe Beatrice had left behind something, a clue, anything that would lead to her current location.

Chapter 8

Hamish sat at the bar in a little Irish pub nestled at the base of a giant hotel. The tiny slice of home in the middle of Philadelphia skyscrapers eased his weary soul.

Murphy's Pub was an old-fashioned, family-owned anomaly right in the heart of Philadelphia. It was also not that far from where Jillian had spent several hours this afternoon.

Hamish had wanted to follow her, but he knew that if he didn't give her a little space, he'd never be able to convince her to work with him. Oh, he had the address where she was at, an apartment building within walking distance of this tiny little pub, which just happened to be walking distance from their hotel.

The bartender wiped the already clean counter in widening circles and smiled at Hamish. "You need another?"

Hamish had been nursing the same lager for the past hour. He checked his phone—the tracking device was still working, and Jillian was on the move. "I'll have to take a rain check."

"You want to settle up then?" The bartender went to the bronze cash register and punched in Hamish's single beer and the order of fish and chips. As he handed Hamish the bill, the door flew open with a frigid gust of wind.

The bartender's eyes lit up with interest. "Now there's a posh one." His accent reminded Hamish of home. In the Outer Hebrides, the line between Scot and Irish was thin.

Hamish turned around to look, struck again by the appearance of the woman he'd been tracking all day. But he played it cool.

Jillian faltered for a moment. Then she continued on, striding right up to him at the bar. She narrowed her gaze and looked at him suspiciously.

He lifted his hands in the air, holding them up in surrender. "What?"

"Why are you here?"

"Just looking for a little place that would remind me of home."

She tapped her foot impatiently and cocked her head, thinking it through.

"I was here first." Hamish pulled out cash and handed it to the bartender. "So now I'm wondering if *you* followed *me*."

Jillian huffed out of breath and all the starch left her. She removed her bright red peacoat then hung it on a peg along with her fancy bag. Surprising them both, she hitched up on the bar stool next to him.

"What can I get you?" The bartender waited with an interested smile.

Hamish guessed white wine, maybe a fancy cocktail.

"I'll take a Guinness."

"Coming right up." He pulled the stout expertly, building the layers slowly in the glass. "Menu?"

At that moment her stomach rumbled. Loudly.

"I'll take that as a yes." He handed her a menu that had been resting between a napkin box and a line of condiments. "Here you go."

Hamish wondered if he should say anything or just wait for her to talk. The bartender placed the perfectly poured Guinness in front of Jillian, and she took a long draw. She set the glass back down on the bar with a clunk. Then tilted her head back and closed her eyes, displaying the elegant line of her neck. Her sigh was more exhale than anything but carried weariness that was evident.

"So how was your day?"

She visibly tightened up, then set her mouth in an unsmiling line. "Frustrating."

Well if that wasn't an answer he didn't want to hear. She wasn't lying, the defeat that she tried to hide was clear. So she hadn't found Brianna.

"I'm sorry to hear that." And he was. More sorry than she would know. If only he could catch a break. He only had a few days left to find Brianna and then he had to figure out what to do with her.

"We could work together." He couldn't help but ask again.

Jill shook her head. "I don't know what you're talking about."

"That's getting a bit old, love."

"I can't."

Well, that was a step forward. At least now she admitted, indirectly, that she was looking for Brianna too.

"If you agree to bring me in," Hamish said, "I will share my information with you."

"You already gave us the information."

"Not all of it."

"Seriously?" Jillian's gray eyes sparkled with irritation. "What kind of information?"

A glimmer of hope fluttered through him. Maybe all was not lost. He had intel that could aid in finding Brianna but he needed leverage so that Jillian Larsen didn't try and ditch him. He'd have to play this very carefully.

"Agree to work with me first." Hamish ran his finger down his bottle of Smithwick's and hoped with more anticipation than was advisable that she would agree.

"I can't do that."

"This is ridiculous. We're going round in circles and we both want the same thing."

"And what is that?" Jill assessed him suspiciously.

Okay, maybe she was right. They didn't want exactly the same thing, but it was close. And that wistful tone in her voice triggered a knowing deep inside him. He opened his emotions and his heart and listened. "We will be stronger together."

They both had pieces of the puzzle needed to find Brianna. Hamish had the compiled intelligence, data only he knew, and Jillian had the resources to put his intelligence together with what they knew.

"Let's call a temporary truce." Jill smiled. "At least while I drink my beer."

"Here's something for free." Hamish gripped the long neck of the beer bottle and didn't look at Jillian. "Brianna probably didn't just steal from the drug centers." His fingers whitened and he forced the truth out between lips gone numb from rage and fear. "She was likely either selling or facilitating the sale of drugs to the patients."

"What?" Jillian drew back away from him as if he'd slapped her. "You can't know that."

"If you look at the statistics, the drug rehab centers in

her case had an unusually high recidivism rate and an unusually high overdose rate."

Jill shook her head in denial. "Addiction is notoriously difficult to cure."

"It's what she did in the UK," he insisted.

"There was nothing about that in the trial information that you gave me."

"I know. This is the new information."

"How do you know?"

"She was arrested for dealing as a youth, and the charge was taken off her record in exchange for community service."

"Fine. But—" Jill pursed her lips "—that could just be supposition. Or dumping the crime on someone who had already been implicated."

"No. I discovered her name in the journal of a former rehab center patient in Northern Ireland."

"How do you know that information is even valid?" Jill argued. "The patient could've been lying."

"He wasn't lying," he said tightly. She kept pushing back, pushing back. Why wouldn't she just believe him?

"How do you know?"

He'd had it. "Because he was my brother!"

He hadn't meant to reveal that.

Unexpectedly, Jillian Larsen's cold gray eyes warmed and the lines on her face softened with sympathy.

His heart clenched. Dammit, he missed his brother.

Jillian Larsen placed her soft elegant fingers over his forearm. And squeezed gently. "I'm so sorry." Her gaze held an unexpected compassion.

Hamish's throat tightened and he swallowed cutting his gaze away from her. Grief was never far from his mind. He hadn't been paying attention. And for that he would never forgive himself.

"What makes you sure it was her?"

"Are you fucking serious?"

"I have to ask."

"At his rehab center they required the patients to keep a journal. And in his journal he mentioned that Brianna tempted him with drugs."

She drew back, shocked. "That's…evil."

"That's what I've been trying to tell you." Hamish signaled to the bartender, who brought over another Smithwick's with a smile. Hamish took a long draw on his beer, trying to ease the ache in his chest and compose himself before he went on.

Jillian asked, "What was she doing there?"

"She continued to 'volunteer,' saying she'd learned the error of her ways."

"Why didn't they ever catch her?"

"That's the question." Hamish said, "Her family was very well connected. They had members of law enforcement on the take who kept them from being arrested. That's why her defection was such a big deal. They'd never been able to catch them."

"Was your brother…involved with her?"

"I don't believe so."

"But she lured him back to his addiction."

"She has a very persuasive personality. She uses her charisma to sway people…the jury, the system. The only people who didn't seem to fall under her spell were her family."

But that still didn't change the fact that she was responsible for his brother's death.

JILLIAN'S HEART ached at the pure grief in Hamish Ballard's eyes.

She wanted to soothe him, comfort him. The emotions were so unexpected that when she clasped his forearm, she squeezed and didn't let go for quite a bit.

He was strong and sinewy beneath her palm. The urge to run her hand up his arm had her pulling away in surprise.

Jillian's cell rang, interrupting their conversation. She glanced at the display, intending to ignore the call but it was Kita and she needed to talk to her. "Excuse me. I have to take this."

"Quite right." Hamish shifted his body so he faced the long bar and stared at the rugby game on the television as if he was grateful for the interruption. But his expression turned even more morose.

"Hey, Kita."

The voice on the other end was strained. "Hey, Jill. You want the good news?"

"Sure."

"Alex and I are enjoying a lovely, chilly day at the Cape."

Kita's clear exasperation made Jill chuckle. Only Kita could make a vacation sound like work.

"What's the bad news?"

"Marsh's Cape house has clearly been closed up for a few months. I don't believe he has been back here since that first week in September."

Jill's shoulders slumped. So Marsh had gone to the Cape and then he'd come to Philadelphia.

Beatrice Winter had disappeared, left town without a trace.

"Do you want the rest of the bad news?" Kita asked.

"There's more?" Jill didn't want to hear it. But she pulled on her big girl panties and braced for whatever Kita was going to say next.

"Marsh called Beatrice's burner a week after we relocated her."

"Do you have the exact time stamp on that?" Because Jill had to wonder about the timing of everything. Had Marsh called Beatrice and she bolted? Or had he called her to arrange a rendezvous?

Marsh had come looking for Beatrice Winter, according to the landlord. The question was, did Beatrice disappear and then Marsh found her? Or was Marsh still looking for her? Or, the one that crept into her brain without permission…did Marsh call Beatrice so they could meet up and disappear together?

Had Beatrice Winter persuaded Marsh to follow her? Just like she'd influenced the jury in her trial in Britain? Just like she'd persuaded Hamish's brother? Who else had her charisma worked on? The CFO, like Hamish claimed?

"Anything else?"

"Yeah. There was an empty bottle of Johnny Walker Blue Label on Marsh's counter."

Jill inhaled. That was Marsh's brooding drink.

"And his fridge was full of French cheese that he didn't open."

They both knew what that meant. Marsh got in funks occasionally. Both she and Kita had coaxed him out of a mood before.

And he'd left the cheese? Not a good sign.

"You need anything else from me right now?" Kita's voice had roughened with frustration and worry.

She started to say no, then paused. "I have company."

"Who? Marsh? Why didn't you say so."

"No." She knew Hamish was listening. "Hamish Ballard."

Kita hesitated. "He's in Philadelphia. He followed you?"

"Bugged the office."

"I knew I liked this guy." Kita laughed softly. "So…what are you going to do?"

"Do?"

"Go for it," Kita urged.

"Not ideal." For multiple reasons.

"Sometimes bad ideas turn out to be the most excellent ones."

When Jill didn't respond, Kita said, "Seize the moment, Jill. You never know when it will come along again."

Her heart warmed, expanded at the possibilities. "Enjoy your weekend with Alex." Jill would carry on here.

"You're sure you don't need me for anything?" So much hope in that question, as if Kita wanted to leave.

That damn urge to see if Kita needed someone to listen prodded her to ask, "Are you and Alex…getting along okay?"

"Sure. Yes." She sighed. "We're good. Great actually. I'm just feeling guilty about taking time off when you're still dealing with all this stuff, and I want you to enjoy yourself for a change."

Jill could hear Alex in the background grumbling, "Kita, seize the moment."

"I'll seize something." Kita threatened. "Any information from Beatrice?"

Hamish was watching the television, but she knew he was listening. His shoulders had tightened when she'd mentioned his name. Every new revelation about Beatrice only underscored that their client had lied to them all. And she was not the woman they'd believed her to be.

He deserved the truth.

Not the whole truth of course. He didn't have to know that ALIAS was responsible for creating her new life. But she could reveal that Beatrice was no longer in Philadelphia.

"No. Beatrice abandoned her apartment in Philadelphia about ten weeks ago." Beside her, Hamish's whole body stiffened. "I went through her apartment today to look for any clues to where she went."

"So you're saying she *is* missing?"

"It would appear so." Although *missing* wasn't really correct. *Hiding* might be a better word.

"Huh, so I guess the Scottish Hottie was right."

"It would appear so," Jill agreed again.

"You sure you don't need me to come down and check it out?" Kita asked.

"No. I've got this."

"Okay, then I'll make nice with my boyfriend." Kita giggled. "It's good to have a marshal in our pocket. And Jill, thanks for sharing."

Jill punched the end button on her phone and waited. Because she just given Hamish Ballard a clue.

He turned to face her and she braced for his condemnation.

The disappointment, the sheer grief on his face, only deepened her remorse. She didn't owe him anything. And yet…she wanted to help him. Understood the emotion that drove him to seek justice for his brother.

He didn't even say I told you so and he would be fully justified in saying so. The weight of everything she'd learned today pressed in on her. She wanted to drown her worry in stout. Or something even more addictive.

She raised her hand signal to the bartender.

"What can I do for you?"

"I'll take a side salad and an order of fries with a side of mayo." She tried to ignore Hamish sitting beside her, but he was hard to ignore. And he still hadn't spoken about Beatrice. "What?"

Hamish took a sip of his beer, then set it on the polished wood countertop.

"I didn't say a thing."

"But you're thinking it." She took another sip of her beer and mulled things over. She kept coming back to three salient facts. "Loudly."

One: Beatrice Winter was a criminal.

Two: Marsh had disappeared after calling Beatrice after she'd been relocated to Philly.

Three: Marsh had been infatuated with Beatrice. Jill knew with absolute certainty that appearances could be deceiving—after all, everyone believed that she'd let Dominic die.

But the fact was she hadn't heard from Marsh in weeks. He was deliberately not available, which made it suspicious. Dee's words from yesterday hit at Jill again. *Partners never know what we go through.*

The cute bartender placed the salad in front of her with a smile and a quirk of his eyebrow. He was a little too young for her but cute in that "I'll be happy to please you" manner.

Even cuter, out of the corner of her eye Hamish bristled. He pressed his wide blunt palms on the bar and pushed half out of his stool to lean over and whisper in the bartender's ear. Bartender held his hands up by his shoulders and backed away, cutting a quick glance at Jill.

"What did you say to him?"

Hamish shrugged. "I have no idea what you're talking about."

From the other end of the bar the bartender glanced between the two of them curiously.

"Seriously? What did you say?"

He took another sip of his beer. She watched the muscles in his throat work as he composed himself. "A gentleman never takes advantage of a vulnerable lady."

"You had no right—"

"You want me to call him back?" Hamish asked.

"Of course not." That moment she'd considered letting go with the bartender was a fleeting, quick little fantasy. He wasn't what she was looking for.

"That one isn't man enough for you."

"And I suppose you are?"

"Well, love, if you're asking."

"You wish."

"I do wish," Hamish blurted out in a confession that surprised them both.

Jill held her breath. Because she knew with a certainty that couldn't be denied that Hamish Ballard had just uttered the absolute truth.

"Scratch that," he muttered. "Bad idea on all fronts." He took another sip of his beer.

She couldn't help but taunting, "It would be a great way to be bad though."

He choked on his beer, sputtering as his gaze shot to her.

"Crikey, woman." He wiped his palm across his mouth. "Are you trying to kill me?"

"But what a way to go." Jill chuckled.

In that moment, he grinned. The unguarded amusement lit up his face and he appeared much younger.

"How old are you?" she asked without thinking.

"Older every day."

Jillian Larsen placed her hand over his, and the shot of adrenaline from that slight touch dropped into her bloodstream like a hit from a needle. "I'm sorry."

"Not your fault." Hamish worried at the label on the bottle. "There are days when I think I'll never find peace again. And then I feel guilty because my brother will never have that option."

She sucked in a breath at his stark honesty. "Are you okay?"

"I will be."

Her fingers squeezed his fist in commiseration.

The bartender placed her French fries in front of her with a thud, breaking the intense moment, and Hamish turned back to his beer.

"Who were you on the phone with?"

"Kita."

"Ah yes, we met in your office." He smirked for a moment, and she wondered what he found so funny. "She's quite the handful."

"She's taken."

"Just an observation, love." He raised a dark eyebrow as if to say *can we get back on task*? "She hasn't heard from your partner?"

She hesitated. "No."

His intensity was compelling. "Has it occurred to you that he's with her. Maybe he's her accomplice."

Jill stiffened. No way would Marsh aid a criminal. He'd been raised in a household that revered the law. His father was a federal judge. And while Judge Robert "Call Me Bobby" Adams was a sexist jerk, he had instilled a strong sense of right and wrong in Marsh.

Of course, Marsh hated his father.

"She's attractive and she uses it." He spoke of Beatrice.

"He isn't one to be influenced by a pretty face."

"We're all susceptible sometimes," Hamish countered. "He wouldn't be the first to fall under her charms."

"Not an option." She gritted out.

"How sure are you?"

"Very." But his persistence sparked a niggle of doubt. Jill had let Marsh handle this case. He'd obviously been attracted to Beatrice. She was pretty sure they'd been having sex.

She'd even asked him about having to let Beatrice go when it was time to place her and leave. Marsh had assured her that he had it under control and Jill had believed him.

She'd been wrapped up in damage control from the shooting incident with the Russians earlier in the year. They'd taken on more pure PR clients just to quell the suspicion and the secrecy that had surrounded that clusterfuck.

And she would be absolutely, positively sure of her partner except for two large glaring questions. Why had Marsh taken the file? And why had he disappeared?

"What's wrong?" Hamish asked.

"Nothing." Jillian dredged her French fries through the mayonnaise. If she had been alone, she would have slumped and propped her chin on one fist. But because the Scottish Hottie—*thank you Kita for planting that one in my brain*—was right next to her, she refused to show any weakness. But a wave of self-pity rolled over her. "You certainly don't need to sit here with me." Her back ached with the rigidness of her muscles.

"I'll walk you to your hotel when you're done."

"You don't have to do that." She was a big girl, she could take care of herself.

"A gentleman walks a lady home."

"Who says I'm a lady?"

His quick grin caused a flutter deep in her belly. Jesus, he was cute. He had broad shoulders, thick thighs, corded forearms, and shoulders that could hold up the world, or keep it at bay.

She was tempted. Disillusioned and disappointed by one of her oldest friends. *Marsh, where the hell are you?* Jill shoved off the bar stool. "Can you watch my stuff for a second?"

"Happy to."

She hustled to the bathroom, furtively pulling her phone from her large bag. Once she was in the small space on the second floor that doubled as a storage closet for toilet paper, paper towels, and other paper goods, she quickly dialed Marsh's cell number.

Jill wanted her old friend to answer. To reassure her that the traitorous thoughts running through her brain were all figments of an imagination gone too long without seeing him. But his phone just rang and rang. Finally, the answering message kicked on. "You've reached Marsh. Leave a message."

Her shoulders slumped and she wondered how much longer she could go on making excuses for him.

"Marsh," she whispered. "I need you to get in touch with me. There's a guy here asking about Beatrice, asking about you. And I've run out of things to stall him with." Jill paused, waited, and then whispered. "I'm losing my faith."

Shit. Guilt swamped her. They had been friends for what felt like forever. They had had each other's backs. Gone through crazy times together. But it seemed like every time Hamish Ballard opened his mouth, Jill had more questions and no answers.

She made her way slowly back down the stairs and headed toward the bar to settle her bill.

She slid onto the bar stool and gestured to the bartender. "Check, please."

Hamish frowned at her. "Aren't you going to finish your dinner?"

She looked down at the food, the grease from the fries congealing in her stomach. Even the fresh salad no longer looked tempting. "Not hungry."

The bartender placed a check on the counter and she pulled out her black credit card. This trip was off the books and she was using her own personal card. No way did she want any of this tied to Adams-Larsen.

Hamish Ballard was watching her with a puzzled expression. His intense regard unsettled and annoyed her. If they had met under different circumstances, she might have asked him out for a drink. But right now all those unspoken and hidden secrets made that impossible.

She quickly settled the bill and gathered her bag and coat.

"Where are you staying?" He crooked a brow at her.

"As if you didn't know."

"Right then." Hamish nodded. "Let me walk you back."

"You don't have to do that."

"But I want to."

"Seriously, you don't."

"The way I see it. We have two options. One: I can escort you back your hotel and we can converse like two mature adults."

"Or?"

"Or two: you can walk to your hotel and I will skulk along behind you, making sure that you arrive safely."

"Skulk?" For some reason, that amused her.

"In a nonthreatening manner, of course."

She laughed, just a little. "Of course."

"Now, are you going to let me escort you or do I have to follow you like some creeper?"

She would admit, only to herself, that she wanted him to escort her. Her feet hurt. Her stomach was still rumbling. And her heart was heavy with all the doubts and questions surrounding her old friend.

Hamish could tell he had her. He crooked his elbow and waited for her to thread her hand through it.

"Escort it is."

"Shall we, milady?"

And that was how she ended up walking back to her hotel with him.

Jill had valeted her car at the hotel and left her bag with the bell captain earlier. She wasn't even sure what had compelled her out into the streets of Philadelphia. The logical choice would have been to check in and order room service. Instead, she'd wandered to the pub.

The walk was quick, only about ten minutes. Once they got to the lobby, Hamish Ballard disappeared with a courtly bow.

She would admit that she had sort of been hoping he would stick around. Okay, truth to tell, she craved *his* company.

She watched him saunter out the exit doors and then turned her attention to the young man behind the front desk. After she checked in, she headed toward the mirrored elevator tucked away in the corner.

While she was waiting for the elevator. Hamish appeared again.

"Now you're skulking?"

"Of course not. I'm staying here as well." He held up a paper bag gripped in one fist. "Nightcap?"

Jill was tired. Really tired. And discouraged and wondering what had happened to her world. The very last person she should have a drink with was Hamish Ballard. Once upon a time she had been bold, fearless, vibrant. But lately her identity had been shaken by the loss of her foundation. She knew he wanted things from her. She knew he believed Marsh was guilty of something. And suddenly she was pissed at Marsh. Would it have been so difficult for him to drop a quick text? To just freaking reassure her that he was still there, that he hadn't abandoned her and their company?

Screw it. "I'd love to."

"Really?"

Ha. She had done the unexpected. And it felt damn good. "You turning me down?"

"Never." The air around them shimmered with tension as his gaze swept over her lingering on her mouth. He vowed, "I will always say yes."

———————————————

Chapter 9

———————————————

The elevator dinged announcing the car's arrival.

"Into the lift with you." He punched the button for the same floor as her room. Jill could give him a hard time or she could let it go. And because she wanted a drink and some company and maybe a flirty conversation, she didn't give him a hard time.

After dumping her bag and briefcase in her room, which conveniently or coincidentally was just down the hall from his, she headed to Hamish Ballard's hotel room. Maybe this was a bad idea. And she certainly didn't want him in her room. This way she could leave whenever she wanted.

Jill knocked on the door, banged really.

He opened it so quickly he must have been hovering, waiting. "I thought you might change your mind."

"I considered it." But here she was.

He unscrewed the cap of the bottle of Balvenie 17 and poured a generous inch and a half into two water glasses. He handed her a glass, then lifted his and clinked them together. "Here's to justice."

She wondered if this was some new tactic. "Are you trying to get me drunk?"

"Certainly not," Hamish said. "But I would like to get to know you better."

"Why?" Jill blurted out rather ungraciously. She watched him, and he was getting ready to spin a lie. "Don't."

"Okay, pure honesty. You're an attractive woman." Hamish took a sip of his whisky, clearly savoring the burn. "Under other circumstances, in another time and place, I would ask you out."

A sense of loss shimmered in front of her. Because there was no other time and place, "There's only now."

"Let's pretend…that we met while I was on holiday."

She wanted to draw out this mellow truce between them so she smiled. "Okay." She took another sip, the rich-bodied liquor burning all the way down.

"So what's the one thing I shouldn't miss in this fair city of Philadelphia?"

"Liberty Bell. Independence Hall. Oh, here's a good one, the haunted prison, Eastern State Penitentiary."

"So my choices are symbols of you Yanks and your successful disentanglement from the Crown—" he laughed just a bit "—or the prison where said Crown would toss you if they found out you were plotting against them."

"All good points." She smiled. "But good reasons to visit here."

Hamish sobered. "I've only one reason to be here." He took a gulp of the expensive scotch.

Since he brought it up, rather than keep it light, she asked the question that had been lingering in her mind. "How did your brother become addicted?"

And there was a way to stop the conversation dead.

He hung his head, avoiding her gaze.

"Sorry. I shouldn't have asked."

"He…played rugby." Hamish circled his glass, watching the liquid swirl. "Got injured when he was tackled, needed knee surgery, got hooked on painkillers, and when the doctor quit prescribing them, he looked for less legal ways to numb his pain."

Jill's heart clenched. "I'm sorry."

"It's a sad, familiar story."

"It doesn't make it any less tragic." She wanted to wrap her arms around him and give him peace. That urge took her by surprise. She wasn't what you'd call a warm, fuzzy person. She tended to be fairly matter-of-fact. Sometimes life sucked, and then you moved on. But she found she wanted to comfort him.

But she held back.

"There's shame, you see." Hamish studied his glass, his eyes sad. "A moral failing, that's what most people think about drugs and addiction." He tipped up his glass and finished it off.

She didn't know what to say so she just kept quiet and took a sip of the liquor savoring the sweet notes of vanilla and winter spice.

"'Just don't start,' people say. My brother—" he paused "—didn't want to admit to our family that he was hooked." He rubbed his blunt-tipped fingers over his face down his cheeks and mouth, holding his hand over his lips as if by stopping what he was going to say, he could stop what had happened. "I didn't even have any fucking idea that he had relapsed."

"I'm sorry." She wanted to comfort him but wasn't sure how. Besides, why would he even want comfort from her?

"He had done his stint at the NHS facility. And it didn't take. So he'd gone to a private facility in Ireland."

Jill kept quiet, letting him talk.

"So the worst thing was I was too busy barreling through my own life, trying to rack up credits and move to the next level." Hamish laughed bitterly. "I was so busy catching those criminals, I didn't even realize that he was drowning."

She couldn't stand it any longer. The whisky flowed through her, warming her from the inside out. She sat on the bed next to him, her thigh along his, their hips touching as she placed her fingers over his wrist. "It wasn't your fault."

He didn't look at her. "I know whose fault it was."

His zeal for catching Beatrice made so much more sense. His pulse thudded against her fingertips, quickening as she unconsciously stroked his skin, wanting to give him solace.

Heat rose between them. When she registered how close they were, Jill glanced up into his navy eyes and the heat nearly incinerated her.

She should move away, retreat from that inconvenient attraction. But she didn't want to. Her breath caught as he very deliberately leaned around her and set his nearly empty glass on the nightstand next to the bed.

His scent, a soft pine that reminded her of Christmas morning, wrapped around her. "You sure you know what you're about, love?" He had curved his arm around her shoulders, the weight solid.

His rough voice, that rolling burr, like a siren lured her into bad choices. "I got nothing."

He carefully lifted her glass from her grasp and placed it next to his on the end table. "Now would be a good time—"

She pressed her fingertips over his lips so that he couldn't finish his sentence. She didn't want to hear what he had to say. Because they both knew this shouldn't happen. But in that moment, the hushed atmosphere of that impersonal hotel room, she needed intimacy. And he needed comfort.

This didn't have to mean anything, it was one step removed from a bar pickup.

If you ignored the fact that they were on opposite sides of the issue of Beatrice. But Jill didn't want think about that right now.

His lips moved beneath her fingertips, but he didn't speak, instead he pursed them and traced his tongue along her fingers.

Jill shivered at the intimate touch. His hand came up and curled around her fingers. Spreading his palm flat against hers, he threaded their fingers together, his right hand, her left, and held on.

Hamish tilted his head and bent toward her. He paused, their lips separated only by a sliver of light and the soft sough of breath.

She let her eyes drift closed and waited. He inhaled, seeming to stop breathing altogether, and she knew this was up to her. Ever so gently, she touched her lips to his. His mouth was hard, yet his touch soft when she fused her lips to his and kissed him.

Jill's heart beat so hard. This moment felt significant, important. As if taking a step that couldn't be reversed. One that would put them on a new path.

He cupped the back of her neck with his left hand, his thumb grazing her jaw as he took over the kiss.

It started out soft, gentle, hesitant, but like lightning, desire exploded between them.

Hamish leaned back against the headboard, drawing her

with him until she lay half over his chest, his pectorals supporting her, a safe place to land.

His fingers tunneled into the twist at her nape, threading through the strands and loosening her hair from the tight clasp.

She tested the muscles of his shoulder, smoothing over his biceps and trailing down his forearm.

Everything about this encounter should be wrong. But instead she felt as if she were coming home. His body cradled hers, his arms tight around her, and his embrace was sure and forgiving.

Her pencil skirt was not conducive to climbing his body the way she wanted to. In a slick move, he rolled onto his back, pulling her with him until their crotches aligned and his thick erection pressed into her belly.

Jillian was a little bit buzzed. Just enough to relax but not so much that her judgement was impaired. This was probably a bad idea, and yet she didn't care.

Hamish was doing very interesting things with his tongue as he pressed a line of kisses along her jaw. He traced the whorl of her ear with his nose, and then nipped gently at her lobe.

"This is a terrible idea." Jill reached for his belt buckle.

"Quite right." He trailed his fingertips down her breastbone and then closed his large hand around her breast and squeezed. Her nipple hardened, almost painfully.

She moaned into his mouth and drew the belt from its loops. Her knuckles brushed his impressive erection, and he plucked at her hardened nipple with renewed enthusiasm.

"Harder, love."

She struggled with his zipper, his erection filling the space like a divining rod bursting toward her and her needy, greedy pussy.

He tugged the dove-gray sweater above the flat plane of her belly and skimmed those calloused fingers along her ribs. Jill's breath caught in her throat. His fingers were sure and confident as he squeezed her lace-covered breast.

He softened his touch, until his fingers were barely there, just lightly stroking the edge of lace.

"Harder, love," she demanded. He laughed into her mouth and scooped her breasts out of the soft lace, but he didn't unclasp her bra, so the mounds pushed up like a feast for the gods.

"You want it hard?" He deftly unbuttoned the waist of her skirt and rolled until she was beneath him, his knees bracketing her hips. His hands cupped her bare breasts as he squeezed them together and sucked both her nipples into his mouth.

Jillian arched up, pressing into his hungry, voracious kiss.

She couldn't spread her legs because they were trapped in the confines of her skirt. Dammit, why'd she pick today to wear her signature skirts?

Jillian groaned, unable to do more than arch against him. He was bent over her, his dark hair flopping in his eyes, and a sheen of sweat shimmered on his brow. His mouth was slick from eating at her. She couldn't stand it and reached into his pants to grab his cock. She wanted him inside her, now.

"Now," she demanded.

He groaned, burrowing his fingers beneath the tight waistband of her skirt.

"No time." Jill didn't want to let go of him. His girth was hot and smooth in her hand as she pumped his dick. A drop of pre-come heated her palm. She commanded him, "Pull my skirt up."

Hamish stood up on his knees, his cock pointing toward

her as she worked him with both hands. He groaned and eased her skirt up over her hips until it was bunched around her waist.

"You're killing me, love."

"Then you can die happy." Jill panted with the frantic need to have him inside her. "Get rid of my thong."

A ruddy flush spread over his cheekbones as he shoved her panties down to her ankles with a deft move. She used her feet to get out of the lace and spread her legs.

"Aren't you a pretty picture?"

"You don't really need to charm me right now." She pumped his cock again, wanting him inside her more than she wanted her next breath. "I'm pretty much a sure thing at this point."

"Maybe so." But he tugged away from her and slithered down her body. "But I want to explore."

"What?" She was a damn sure thing. "Where are you going?"

He placed his hands back on her breasts. Her clothes sort of still on, her skirt rucked around her waist and her sweater shoved up around her collarbones.

He played with her sex, stroking into her with his sure callused fingers. Her body responded to him as he conducted her arousal, playing her body like a finely tuned instrument. He plucked at her nipples while he devoured her with his mouth. He nipped the soft skin of her thighs and rubbed the scruff from his beard against her as he licked into her with an intimate kiss.

She was trapped by her clothes and he took advantage of the restraints to play with her body, paying sensuous attention to every erogenous zone she'd ever had and some she'd never expected.

Jillian arched up into his embrace as her orgasm swept

over her in a sudden violent crest. Her sex contracted in bright sharp spasms, milking his fingers and throwing her body into a slipstream of sensation. She moaned his name, wanting to touch him, feel his body press down on hers.

Hamish continued to kiss her and stroke her body, slowly easing her through the intense sensations until her heart rate slowed and her body came down from the high.

She sat up quickly and shoved his pants to his knees. He was right there in front of her and she licked her lips, leaning forward, ready to inhale him, as he had inhaled her.

He reached for his wallet and pulled out a condom. Before she could do more than lap at him a few times, he had rolled the condom on and edged over her.

He paused at the entrance to her body, the tip of his cock nudging her swollen lips.

"You sure, love?"

"Has anyone ever told you that you talk too much?"

"I'll take that as a yes."

He took his time, easing into her body with finesse. Her sensitized channel, swollen and aroused, accepted him greedily into her body.

They were both holding their breath as if waiting in anticipation for something neither of them had expected.

"We good?" He was seated to the hilt inside her, invading her with his masculinity. He was nearly flush with her body but still kept his upper body propped on his elbows so that he didn't crush her. A gentleman even during sex.

They lay there connected in the most intimate of ways. Still he didn't move and just let her body adjust to his size.

He fit. They fit.

He pulsed within her and she arched up into him, demanding without words.

Finally. Finally, he began stroking in and out of her body

with muscled ease. The dusting of hair on his chest rubbed at her already sensitized nipples. Jillian wiggled a little and wrapped her legs around his thighs, pushing up into him with every thrust.

With every rock of his hips, he hit that spot inside her, and her desire began to build again.

Hamish grunted and slid his hands beneath her ass and cupped her in his palms.

He canted her hips and began to power into her until they were banging together in a frantic rhythm. Every hit of her G spot and the tingles grew, flowing over her body, into her, out of her like a tsunami until her orgasm battered at her and she tumbled head over heels into another realm.

Above her Hamish stiffened, his neck and face straining as his orgasm crashed into him. She didn't usually watch her partners when they came. But there was something beautiful and magnetic about the way that he let the sensations overwhelm him.

With a muffled groan, he collapsed on top of her, his face buried in the curve of her neck, he licked her skin, tracing the same path as before, and then nipped at her earlobe. And their hearts slowed together in a beautiful rhythm.

Jillian hadn't let go with a man in a very, very long time.

Maybe she should be sorry she'd chosen Hamish, but she wasn't.

HAMISH NUZZLED the curve of her neck.

His heart thundered in a furious beat. The interaction had been quick and frantic. For round two he'd like to take his time. Explore her body and her reactions in more depth.

But he had no idea if she'd shove him out of bed, figuratively of course since they were in his bed.

He wasn't sure what to say. He didn't want to break this fragile truce. But they needed to talk and he had a feeling that the sex wasn't going to ease the issues between them.

"That was—"

She placed her fingertips over his lips. "No regrets."

Hamish's brows rose. In his experience, even when people wanted no regrets some were inevitable. "Sounds good." And he pursed his lips and kissed hers.

"Now you're quiet," she teased.

"You're the one talking too much at the present." He nuzzled her neck, pressing soft openmouthed kisses along her collarbones and gearing up for round two.

"I just had two orgasms." She certainly wasn't shy. "And you…you can't possibly—"

He lifted his head, to see her surprised expression. She gave a soft laugh when he began to harden.

Flirty, she smiled at him, her lips curving. She looked…happy.

"With the right incentive, I absolutely positively can."

Jillian said, "Then let me put my mouth to better use and give you incentive."

And she did.

Chapter 10

Jillian lay in the hotel room bed, thinking about all the reasons why last night had been a bad idea. But the thing she kept going back to was…it had felt good. Better than good. She had taken a few hours for herself, indulging her inappropriate attraction to Hamish.

But it was a new day and she needed to get going.

"Good morning," Jillian rasped in husky post-sex voice.

Hamish rolled over and propped his head on his palm, his bare chest distracting her. He smiled lazily, his surprisingly even teeth gleaming white in the dim, shadowed light of the hotel room. "Brekkie, love?"

"We had a good time last night." She pushed up from the bed and a rush of cold air swept between them. "Doesn't mean we're best buddies today."

"I thought you said no regrets."

"Just because I don't have any regrets doesn't mean I'm suddenly going to trust you."

"Fine, then let's talk about the elephant we ignored last night. Your partner is involved with Brianna."

Her mouth hardened. "You don't know that."

And they were back to being enemies. The truce had been nice, but the truth was they were on opposite sides of this…problem.

"Even though it's circumstantial, it is fairly damning."

"How can you say that?"

He ticked off the facts on his fingers. "Your partner is missing. Brianna aka Beatrice is missing."

"That doesn't mean together." Jill shook her head and left the bed completely naked.

"Can you verify that they disappeared about the same time?"

Jill refused to be self-conscious about her nude body. She started picking up pieces of clothing.

She clipped her bra together. Hamish watched with hot eyes, and she wished that the soft woman who woke in his arms had time for another round. But her hardheaded take-no-prisoners business persona was back. She had to protect her heart from hurt.

"Still doesn't mean they're together." She was pissed.

"Let's work together and you can prove me wrong," Hamish coaxed. His charming grin almost worked on her.

The ringing of her cell, an old-fashioned dial telephone ring, muffled and barely audible interrupted their…discussion.

The ringing stopped.

Jillian pulled her phone from the pocket of her Hermès leather bag. The missed call was from Jake. She was about to hit redial when her phone began ringing again. Jake. She pressed the answer button. "This is Jillian."

"Hey, Jill, bad news." Jake's voice was tight and annoyed.

She pulled out her earphones and plugged them in.

"Hit me." Jill reached for her underwear, irrationally

feeling more self-conscious now that she was on the phone. Standing on one foot, she slipped on the impractical thong and tugged it up one-handed, only pausing when Jake said, "Somebody tried to break in."

"Tried?"

"Yeah. They weren't subtle about it either."

"Did the security system get any good photographs?"

"I'm going through the feed as we speak." Jake sighed. "We're going to need a new back door."

"I can be there in a few hours."

There was a pause. "Hours?"

The only one in the office who knew she'd gone to Philadelphia was Kita.

"Uh, yeah. Sorry, I'm…out of pocket." Jill began scrolling through airline websites to get a new flight back to DC.

"Everything okay?" The sleep-riddled voice of last night's mistake interrupted her search for her blouse. Hamish stood in front of her. His chin dipped low as he searched her face.

"Who's that?" Jake said in her ears.

"Everything is fine." Jill glanced at her screen again, then checked the time. There was an 8 a.m. flight she could make if she rushed. "I'll be back soon."

"Everything okay there, Jill?" Jake asked again.

"It will be." Jill stood in the middle of the hotel room. Half clothed in only her underwear, she pawed through the pile of clothing on the floor. "See you soon."

She tucked her phone into the back pocket of her skirt and slipped her arms through yesterday's sleeveless sweater.

"Anything I can do to help?"

Last night's distraction was today's annoyance. But a thought did occur to her. "Did you come here alone?"

Hamish jerked back. "What's that supposed to mean?"

"To the United States? Alone?"

A flash of something flickered then disappeared in his dark blue eyes.

"Someone tried to break into our offices." Jill narrowed her gaze at him. "Awfully convenient that you show up asking questions and a couple days later my office is compromised."

"You don't seriously think that I had anything to do with that." He propped his hands on his hips, the very picture of male outrage. *Naked* male outrage. "I've been in Philadelphia, with *you*, for the last 24 hours."

Well, that was one way to get rid of her one-night stand. Accuse him of a crime.

"You're right. Forget it." Except he hadn't confirmed coming to the States alone.

She shrugged on her matching cardigan, buttoning it up quickly and trying to forget last night when he had been undressing her. The sensual glide of his fingertips over her lace-clad skin, his knuckles brushing her nipples as he had facilitated a mini striptease.

"Got to go." She walked into her pumps and headed toward the door. She tried unsuccessfully to ignore him.

"I'm coming with you."

"I don't think so."

"So we're back to this?"

"I guess we are." She should never have forgotten that he was the enemy. And though he denied it, she had to wonder if the attempted break-in at Adams-Larsen was somehow connected to Hamish Ballard and her missing client.

HAMISH STARTED to throw on his clothes, determined to follow Jillian. But with each piece of clothing he put on, kind of like putting on armor, he realized that he should just let her go. She needed a little time to cool down. Because clearly he had nothing to do with the break-in at her office.

He also wanted to spend a few more hours in Philadelphia. Something Jillian said last night had sparked his thought process. He knew that Brianna had been in Philadelphia and he knew she had been close by. He had gone into an Irish pub for a little taste of home. Maybe she had the same impulse. So he packed up his things, checked his bag with the bell captain and headed back to Murphy's pub.

Hamish walked into the pub, the dark interior warm and welcoming, and evoking memories of his favorite pub back home. He sat down at the bar and smiled at the bartender from last night.

"You're here again?" Hamish asked.

"Family owned. We all work long hours." He shrugged. "Same as yesterday?" the bartender asked, grabbing a bottle of Smithwick's and getting ready to pop it open.

"You've a good memory."

"Pays to remember your customers' preferences."

"True. But I was only in here once."

"I never forget a face."

Could it really be that easy? Hamish nodded. "Actually today I'll take a Guinness."

Going on a hunch, he reached into his satchel and pulled out a photograph of Brianna. "Has she ever been in here?" He held the picture of Brianna toward the bartender.

The guy set his Guinness on the bar, the head of foam a perfect pour. He reached out his hand and Hamish placed the picture in it. The guy held it up to his face. "She does look familiar." He squinted at the picture for longer. "Okay, yes. But she had brown hair when she was here."

"Do you recollect how long ago she was here?" Hamish's blood quickened, and his heart began a rapid tattoo. This guy had actually seen Brianna in this bar. This felt like a big step forward.

"Would've been in the summer. She was always wearing dresses. She had a very nice baps." The guy gestured to his chest. Brianna Walsh was very well endowed.

"Did she have an accent?"

"Not a strong one, but there were hints."

"So, she came in more than once?" Hamish considered that. Brianna had a weakness. A longing for home.

"She was here every day for about a week." The bartender propped his elbow on the bar, settled his chin on his fist. He sighed. "And then one day she said goodbye."

Hamish sat up straight in in his bar stool. "Did she say where she was going?"

"North. She sat in the corner with her Bulmers Pear Cider and a train schedule on the counter."

Hamish wondered how personal he could get, then figured fuck it. He needed to know where she went. "Don't suppose you know where she was going?"

The bartender narrowed his gaze at Hamish. "You seem like a nice enough bloke, but how do I know you don't mean her harm?"

"You are right." And he couldn't lie because the truth was he wanted her in prison for her crimes. He wanted her to pay for killing his brother. Even if she hadn't shoved the needle into his brother's arm, she had given him the means to overdose. "Hate to break it to you, mate. But she's a criminal."

The bartender raised his eyebrows. "Seriously?"

"Yep. I've been tracking her from the UK."

"Well, isn't that a kick in the pants." The bartender shook his head. "You could be lying."

"I could be. But I'm not." He flipped open his wallet and showed the bartender his warrant card that identified him as an NCA officer and included his picture.

"Ballard? I thought you looked familiar." He glanced at the television, where yet another rugby game was playing.

A pang of grief hit Hamish.

"You're the spitting image of Charlie—"

"Twins," Hamish said abruptly.

"I'm sorry for your loss." He spoke the simple words quietly.

Hamish nodded. "Thanks."

The bartender cleared his throat and nodded at the picture. "I don't know exactly where she was going, but she seemed to be looking at train schedules from Philadelphia to Portland, Maine." The bartender wiped the already clean bar in rough circles as if deep in thought. Brianna could do that to a man...or a woman.

Hamish tossed down twenty US on the bar and stood to leave. "Thank you for your help."

His hunch had paid off. He now knew that Brianna had left Philadelphia after being here a week and she had headed north. But when he pulled up the Amtrak train schedules on his mobile, he realized there was a lot of territory between Portland and Philadelphia. And she could have stopped at any of those towns. But it was a step in the right direction.

His first thought, his first instinct, was to call Jillian and fill her in. Except she wanted nothing to do with him. And she still wanted to believe that her partner wasn't guilty of colluding with Brianna.

But Hamish understood that Brianna was a user. She used her sexuality and her acting skills to convince people to help her.

She was also memorable. Not the smartest move when on the run.

Which meant that he had to speak with Jillian again, even if she wanted nothing to do with him. And he wanted to share the information he'd just gotten.

Because he was going to need her resources to find Brianna. And he hadn't told her everything.

Chapter 11

Hamish headed to the train station. Yes, it was a long shot but at this point he didn't have any other leads to go on.

His mobile rang and the number looked to be from the Washington, DC area. It wasn't Jillian's cell but still his pulse quickened. Maybe she had changed her mind and decided she could work with him.

He answered quickly. "Hamish Ballard."

"Hello, Mr. Ballard, it's your hostess."

His level of disappointment was disproportionate to his hope. He should've known better.

"Aye. What can I do for you?"

"Are you on your way back to the city?"

He had kept the rental since he wasn't sure how long he would be in Philadelphia, but he had notified his hostess that he wouldn't be there for a day or two. "No. I'm sorry, I am still in Philadelphia."

"Oh dear, oh dear, oh dear."

"What seems to be the problem?"

"I'm sorry to inform you that there's been a break-in."

His temporary landlady let out a sob. "The cops need to ask you some questions."

The American police. Not what he wanted to hear and not the best news. "I didn't leave much there…."

He trailed off. He had brought his clothing with him to Philadelphia. However, the recording equipment for the listening device that he'd placed in Jillian's office was there.

"They really need to speak with you."

Hamish thought quickly. There'd been a break-in at Jillian's office. And there'd been a break-in at his Airbnb. Could the two be connected?

"I'll be there as soon as I can."

Several hours later Hamish surveyed the destruction of his rented flat. Several small things stuck out at once. One: his recording equipment was gone. That could be attributed to a general theft. Two: much of the flat's furnishings had also been destroyed.

"Can you tell me if anything is missing?" The young constable asked Hamish. And no, he bloody well couldn't share with the local police that his illegal surveillance devices had gone missing.

Hamish glanced around the apartment. "I'd only been here a couple of nights." His gaze took in the rage evident in the trashed parlor.

"Can you tell me you've been over the past twenty-four hours?"

Hamish was so busy calculating odds in his head, it took him a moment to process what the constable was asking

"Am I a suspect, then?" He shook his head.

"I'm just trying to rule out the obvious."

"I am an officer at the National Crime Agency here on holiday." But Hamish quickly realized that he certainly did not want his boss to verify his occupation because then she would know that he had disobeyed a direct order and come to the United States. "And I was in Philadelphia."

"Can anyone verify your story?"

Jillian Larsen could. Hamish rubbed his fingers over his right eyebrow over the small cut from Marsh's closet door. "Aye."

"Name and phone number?"

Hamish sighed. He had no other choice. Then another thought struck him. What if she hadn't removed the bug? Whoever had stolen his equipment could be listening to her right now.

He rattled off Jillian's name and her mobile number, which he'd fortunately memorized.

She'd had a break-in at her office. And she'd planned to go there as soon as she got back to DC. What if she'd been attacked once she arrived?

The officer quickly punched in her number. He stared steadily at Hamish as the mobile rang on the other end.

"This is Jillian."

When Hamish heard her voice, his tension eased and he let out the breath he'd been holding.

After a few questions, the cop nodded and got ready to hang up the phone. Hamish's mind had been ticking along as he listened to the cop ask her the same questions and catalogued her answers.

He finally nodded sharply. "Your story checks out."

Of course it did. But Hamish kept his expression calm and polite. No need to piss off the police officer.

"Wait. Before you hang up, can I speak with her?"

The constable hesitated, then nodded. "Mr. Ballard would like to speak with you."

Hamish waited. With Jillian, he never knew what her

response would be. The constable studied him for another second and then handed Hamish his mobile.

"We need to talk," Hamish said to Jillian. "Immediately."

"I'm dealing with some things here right now. It isn't a good time."

Hamish huffed out a breath. "It really can't wait." She started to object again but he had learned his lesson. Instead of trying to convince her, he hung up the phone and handed it back to the police officer. "Thank you for your time and the use of your mobile."

"Good luck," the cop said. "That was one pissed-off woman."

The cop had no idea.

"Are we done here?"

"For now."

Hamish nodded. "Then I'm free to go?"

The constable agreed. "You're free to go, but if you recall anything, any information that might help us determine who did this, please call me." He handed Hamish his card.

Hamish headed for the ALIAS office at a run.

He made it down the street in record time. When he got to the understated brownstone, he rushed up the steps and pressed the video doorbell.

A disembodied voice said, "We're not open for business." Not Jill.

"I need to see Jillian." He *needed* to see her. See for himself that she was okay. He knew the need was irrational. He knew it and still no fucking way was he backing down. The constable had just talked to her and he was mostly sure she was still at her office.

"Come back tomorrow during regular business hours."

He wasn't waiting until Monday morning to confirm that she was okay and hadn't been harmed. Hamish pressed the button again.

"Jillian, I know you're in there." He wanted to pound his fist in frustration at the doorjamb. Instead, he closed his eyes, drew a deep breath, and let it out slowly. "Listen, Mac, I need to speak to Jillian."

Another *longer* pause.

The door buzzed. "Come through the hallway to the back entrance." Her voice. Thank Christ. He grabbed for the door handle, yanking the heavy wood door open quickly, just in case she changed her mind.

Hamish made sure the door closed behind him before he rushed through to the back of the building. He zipped past the workout room, another door he still wasn't sure where it led to, and the former formal dining room that seemed to be set up as a conference room now. When he got to the other side of the building, he finally saw her. That tension that gripped him when he had realized their break-ins were likely connected eased slightly. She was okay.

Other things registered once his irrational fear dissipated. The large black guy with a trimmed Afro and hazel eyes looked up from where he was bent over Jillian. They were very close. Hamish didn't like how close together they were. The territorial feelings zooming through him were unexpected. One night together didn't grant him any rights and yet he still didn't like the implied intimacy.

He didn't have a possessive bone in his body. He was all about the pleasure and not about the aftermath. He'd had his eye on bigger fish than bagging a girl. He'd wanted to move up the ranks at the National Crime Agency, and to do that he had been unwilling to be encumbered by a wife.

He'd always figured he'd get married after he got his career goals out of the way.

He had also thought that he and his fictional girl would spend holidays at his family's home along with his brother.

If life had taught him anything, it was that you had to seize moments when you could.

When the black bloke saw him, he straightened and narrowed his gaze. "Are you sure you want to let him in?"

Jillian placed her hand on the guy's forearm. Those inappropriate and unexpected very territorial thoughts rose again.

"It's fine, Jake," she said huskily.

Hamish wanted to pry her fingers off the very buff man's arm.

They had already placed plywood over the broken glass in the vestibule. But Hamish could see the cracks in the doorjamb. Splinters of stained wood littered the floor as if whoever had tried to get in was enraged.

Kind of like the destruction at his flat. "We need to talk."

Jillian flicked her gaze to the black guy. "We'll be done in a second."

"You want me to wait in your office?"

"Absolutely not. I want you where I can see you at all times."

"Quite right." Hamish tried not to let his disappointment show. She didn't trust him. "Anything I can do to help?"

"We're almost done here."

They put up yellow caution tape while Hamish twiddled his thumbs and covertly studied the easy camaraderie between Jillian and her employee.

"You want me to stick around?" His deep voice rumbled in the silence between Hamish and Jillian.

"He's harmless." Jill smiled softly at the guy and Hamish wanted to punch him in the face. "Thanks for coming in on a Sunday to help take care of this. If you could wait until we're done, that would be optimal."

"Any time, Jill." Jake hesitated once more. "You know I've got your back."

"Thank you."

He shot one more cautionary look at Hamish. "I'll stay on overwatch."

"What was so important that it couldn't wait?" Jillian rolled her eyes at him.

"In your office." Hamish wasn't sharing this information with anyone but her.

Jillian shrugged. "Let's go."

They headed up the grand staircase to her office. She opened the door to her office and Hamish held up a finger to tell her to be quiet.

"Now, what's so important—"

He should have known she wouldn't listen to his directive. So he stopped her the only way he could think of at that moment.

He pressed his mouth to hers. Initially it was just to stop Jillian from giving anything away in case whoever broke into his flat was listening.

But the moment that his lips met hers, the desperate move changed into something more primal. She was okay. He poured all the relief and thanks and emotion that had torn through him when he'd been worried about her into their kiss.

And she must have forgotten that she was pissed at him because she kissed him right back.

She moaned softly, bringing Hamish back. He didn't want anyone hearing those sounds except him. He pulled away gently and whispered in her ear. "Bugs. Someone stole my listening equipment. Worried it's the same perps. Shh."

The hazy look in her gray eyes cleared and she nodded.

Hamish stalked toward her desk. He leaned over and searched for the small bug that he'd placed there, was it only two days ago?

He ran his fingers along the underside of the desk but the device was gone. He crouched down and double-checked in case he'd somehow missed it. But it definitely wasn't there any longer.

She'd had it removed. Hopefully, they'd found the other as well.

Hamish went over to the small seating area and searched for the bug he'd put underneath the coffee table. He triple-checked to make sure he didn't miss it, crouching underneath and lighting up the flashlight app on his phone. But it was gone.

He climbed to his feet slowly. His relief was a physical thing as the panic that had gripped him dissipated. "What did you do with them?"

She grinned evilly. "Flushed."

He winced. Those had set him back. But it was still worth it if he found Brianna Walsh. "Seriously?"

The daze from their kiss had worn off. Except thank Christ she'd had them removed.

"Someone ransacked my flat and stole my recording equipment." He gestured to the office. "Clearly they figured out either from following me or from the recording equipment who I was listening to."

Jill opened her mouth.

Hamish held up his hand again. "They tried to break into your office. You need to leave. Straightaway."

But she didn't make any attempt to move. "Who are *they*?"

"I have no bloody idea."

"You're making assumptions." Jillian crossed her arms over her chest, the posture defensive and he wondered what was going on in that complicated head of hers.

"I'd rather assume and be wrong than ignore the facts in front of us," he shot back.

"I refuse to be run out of my own office."

"Well then, you better have your hulk watching carefully."

"Speculate as to who tried to break in."

Hamish really didn't have any idea. No one was supposed to know he was here. But he couldn't admit that to Jillian.

"I really *don't know*."

WONDERFUL. Hamish was evading her inquiry. Was he lying? Maybe, maybe not. But he was definitely not sharing everything with her.

She might have questioned whether his apartment had been broken into if it weren't for the fact that a cop called her. Of course he could've paid someone to pretend but she didn't think so.

"Give me a minute." Jill rubbed a hand over her forehead, as if trying to ease away a headache. She pressed a button on the office intercom. "Jake. Code yellow while I take this meeting. Be on the lookout for company."

"Wilco."

"I have new information about Brianna, er your Beatrice. I went back to the Murphy's Pub this morning," Hamish said. "The bartender recognized her."

Jill sat up in her chair. "Wait, Beatrice was there?"

"Yes. Apparently she went in every day for a week and then abruptly said goodbye with a train ticket in hand and a final bottle of cider."

"That still doesn't give us any information on where she is now."

"North of Philadelphia."

"That was ten weeks ago. She could be anywhere."

"I had an idea." Hamish cocked a brow at her, hesitated. "Well out with it."

"Brianna is a creature of habit. She missed home. Which got me to thinking about your partner and how to find him."

Jill scrunched up her face. Marsh still had not called her back. And she was really beginning to wonder if maybe he had run off with Beatrice. It was time to trust Hamish Ballard. At least a little.

After all, he wasn't obligated to tell her about Beatrice and the train ticket. It was another data point in the search to find her since she had bailed on their relocation.

"Are you going to share with me?" Hamish asked. "I gave you information about Brianna."

"What do you want to know?" she asked, feeling defeated.

"Your partner is missing," he stated.

She shrugged. Not answering.

"Where have you looked for him?"

Where hadn't she looked? "His usual places."

"No sightings?"

"No."

"Credit card usage?"

She just stared at him.

"Quite right," he said, "You checked."

Shit. He had heard her tell Kita to break the law.

"No information then?"

Marsh hadn't used his company cards or his personal credit cards since two weeks after he left. Which meant he must have Black cards. Unless he had taken out cash. According to Kita, he'd gone to the Cape. He'd come back to DC and then been in Philadelphia. Where they had relocated Beatrice Winter.

Maybe she should be worried that he was dead.

"Would he have a burner phone?" Hamish pulled her out of her musings.

"Likely." Probably more than one.

"We could back-trace from his known contacts and see if an unknown number shows up."

But he would have called her…or Kita. And he hadn't reached out to either of them.

However it was a solid idea.

"What about family members?" Hamish prodded. "Siblings?"

"Only child." Same as her. They'd bonded over that once upon a time.

"Who are his friends?"

"Me. Kita." Kita was Marsh's closest friend. They'd known each other since high school. And Kita would tell Jill if she'd heard from Marsh. Oddly her relationship with Kita had grown closer since Marsh had disappeared.

"Who else is he close to?"

"His mother."

"Has your partner contacted his mother?"

"We checked his cell phone records," Jill admitted

grudgingly. "He hasn't made any calls in the past ten weeks."

"Does his mother live nearby?"

"Yes, but I don't want to worry her." Except maybe it was time to get worried. Hamish just studied her waiting for her come to the same conclusion as him. He was right. "We need to talk to Marsh's mother."

"We can come up with a cover story before we talk to her."

Jill tapped her fingers on the desk blotter. "What if we just check his mother's phone records?"

Because he had a point. If Marsh was using a burner, he would still call his mother. Jill slapped her forehead. Why hadn't she thought of that?

She could ask Kita to check Colleen Adams's cell and landline records. On the sly. But Kita was in Cape Cod and she was their resident hacker.

"I'll have Kita check tomorrow when she gets back."

"Why don't we check now?"

Jill studied him. "That isn't my skill set."

"I am rather handy with a computer." Hamish grinned charmingly. "If you will give me access to your system."

The last thing she wanted to do was give him access to the ALIAS system, but if he were right, they might finally have a lead on Marsh which might lead to Beatrice.

"It will take more than handy."

Hamish sighed. "I work Cyber Crimes, love."

Well, that explained a lot.

Hamish Ballard had slowly wormed his way into her search for Marsh. But this quest had become about protecting her company, not about protecting her client and her partner. Because if Marsh had betrayed her, the only thing she had left was the company.

She had people depending on her for their livelihood. And even more people depending on her to keep them safe.

"Together." He eyed her suspiciously. "We do this together or I won't share."

She nodded shortly. "Fine."

She made him sit on the loveseat until she was signed into their sophisticated tracking system. "Okay, now you can look at it." But she wasn't going to let him have unfettered access. So once Hamish sat in her chair, Jill leaned over his shoulder and watched every move.

He finessed the keys and for a moment Jill was transported back to last night when he had used those fingers to bring her pleasure. Heat swelled over her in a wave.

She needed to forget about last night. It was an aberration. One she couldn't afford to repeat.

"Okay. I'm ready. Give me his mother's phone number."

Jillian gave him Colleen Adams's phone number. Within several minutes her phone records came up. It was going to take a while to eliminate valid phone numbers and see if there were any matches. Hamish hit print and several pages of data chugged out.

"This could take a while." Jillian reached for a pen and scratched out Kita's phone number and her own phone number quickly. Both she and Kita checked in with Colleen regularly.

Another number they could cross out was Judge Adams's. He was her ex-husband and monthly booty call— something Jill tried really hard not to think about.

She highlighted several numbers that occurred regularly. Using their private database to identify phone numbers, Jillian was able to rule out a few more numbers as legitimate businesses.

She should have thought about the fact that Colleen had not seemed worried about Marsh. She would bet that he had been calling his mother this whole time. Which meant that he had purposely not been calling her.

That thought triggered a mix of feelings. Hurt. Why hadn't he called her? Suspicion. Because if he wasn't calling her, did he think he was doing something wrong? Disappointment. The hope that she had been carrying around slowly diminished.

Their office had been compromised. She couldn't afford to ignore Hamish's attempts to work together anymore.

There were only three numbers that they couldn't identify. "If we can check the records and see where the signal pinged from, we could have a lead." The pieces of the puzzle were coming together. She just needed to be patient.

"We're close." Hamish asked distractedly, "What did the police say when you told them about your break-in?"

Silence.

"You didn't tell them?"

"That's not your concern." Jill used her frosty ice-queen voice.

Hamish didn't chastise her but she knew he was thinking it. Which made her uncomfortable. She couldn't read him that quickly, could she?

"Did you get any video of the attempted break-in?"

"Yes." It would help if they knew who had broken in but neither she nor Jake recognized the perpetrators. "If I show you the video recording, can you see if you recognize them?"

"Aye."

They shifted positions, and Jill now sat at the computer.

With a few keystrokes, Jill opened up the five-minute recording. The perpetrators wore ball caps on their heads and gloves on their hands and kept their heads down. But maybe if this was related to Hamish's need to find Beatrice, he would be able to identify the attackers. They were white, fair-skinned. But that was really all that could be seen on the recording.

Jill had already watched with Jake. The sick feeling in the pit of her stomach grew as the rage from the two men became more evident. Toward the end when they couldn't breach the door, the physicality of the crowbar swings against the door jamb were intense. It was clearly not random. And all Jill could think was thank goodness no one had been around to become the target of all that rage.

Hamish leaned over her shoulder, one hand on the back of the chair. The other palm pressed flat on her mahogany desk.

A shiver skittered down her spine.

Hamish's heat surrounded her. She should have felt trapped, but instead a feeling of safety enveloped her.

"Wait." He tapped the keyboard with his fingers stopping the video. "Back that up just a bit."

Jill hit the rewind button at the slow speed and went back ten seconds.

Then she hit play again.

"Stop right there."

Both men had kept their heads down, and the ubiquitous DC tourist caps sold by street vendors shaded their face so that it was impossible to identify them. But Hamish had caught a small mistake. For a brief instant, the face of one man was visible. Hamish drew in a sharp breath.

"You know him?"

Hamish straightened suddenly and propped his hands on his hips. "Bollocks."

Chapter 12

"What does that mean?"

"Nothing good." Shite. Hamish needed to think. What were Matthew and Malachi Walsh doing in Washington, DC? Hamish shoved away from her and paced around her office, making a circle between the grouping of seating and the desk. "That's Brianna's cousin."

"I thought you said her family was in jail?"

"Her father and two brothers," Hamish said shortly. "She decimated their business after they kicked her out. The cousins must be looking for her to find out if she hid money or what she did with all their files."

Because Brianna Walsh hadn't just testified against her family, she had singlehandedly taken apart their business, destroying computer records and closing bank accounts. Hamish had always thought she'd pocketed the money. Or at the very least skimmed off the top. Although according to the file he'd looked at, she had claimed to be broke.

"How did they escape prosecution?"

"The theory was that they were too small to bother with. They personally didn't have the relationships with the higher-up criminal elements. So the government chose to concentrate on putting the main Walsh family away."

"Ugh. I hate expedient choices." Jillian pressed her palms flat on the desktop. "Did they testify against their family?"

"Not a chance. Part of the reason Brianna needed resettlement was to protect her from a hit."

"Do you think they are here to kill her?"

"Malachi is known to be brutal with a knife." The Walsh family was famous for their vicious style of execution, and Brianna's immediate family had been the core of the criminal enterprise. As far as he was aware, neither Malachi or Matthew had killed anyone. However, perhaps the cousins were dirtier than anyone knew. "So…possibly."

"Still, why would they follow you?"

That was the question, wasn't it?

"At the NCA I was vocal in my criticism of Brianna and her need to pay for her crimes." Hamish mulled over the implication of the Walsh brothers in Washington. "Everyone knew I wanted her brought back in."

"You think they followed you here to catch you apprehending her?"

The problem with that was no one was supposed to know he was in the US. Of course, Jillian didn't know that. And he wasn't about to share. "It is more imperative than ever that we find Brianna and Marsh." Before the Walsh family found her.

He wanted her rotting in prison. But he had a feeling that the Walsh cousins had a more permanent solution to her betrayal in mind.

She shuddered.

"You do think they are together?" Jill said, clearly trying to hide her glum tone.

He knew immediately she was referencing her partner and Brianna. "Possibly." Hamish conceded. "I potentially have some other information that might help find her."

"More?" she ground out.

He knew she'd be pissed but…"I couldn't trust you until today." And he still wasn't completely sure he could trust her.

"Fine. What now?"

It was time for him to share. He had the intelligence, and she had the resources he needed. "Brianna needs special medicine."

"What kind?"

"She takes a very specific medicine for partial-onset seizures." That was not common knowledge. "She should be running out soon or have already received the prescription. It's a Class IV drug so if I've understood your prescription drug laws, it should be monitored."

Jillian tapped her foot in a quick staccato rhythm. Her gray eyes narrowed with pure annoyance.

Hamish continued, "If we can confirm your partner's cell phone location, then we can search for pharmacies that dispensed that medicine to female patients in her age range, and we might have a line on her location. We might even be able to narrow it down by new prescriptions issued."

"And you didn't think to share this information sooner?" If anything, she looked more pissed. "I could have been researching this two days ago."

"I wanted to make sure we were truly working together before I gave you that intel."

Hope began to blossom. In any good investigation, there was always a tipping point at which all the pieces started to come together and form a complete picture.

Hamish had backtracked through the calls made by the

mobile number that they believed could be Marsh Adams's but it wouldn't hurt to confirm the number with the man's mother.

"Can you call his mother and ask about the phone number we've got?"

After an awkward few minutes on the phone, Colleen Adams confirmed that the number she had received calls from every two weeks was in fact her son's.

Jillian hung up the phone, looking unexpectedly defeated.

"You okay?"

"I will be." She straightened her shoulders.

Hamish had been so caught up in moving forward in his own quest, that he'd forgotten that Marsh Adams meant something to her.

He wanted to apologize but he wasn't sorry.

It appeared more and more probable that Marsh Adams was in the middle of something nefarious. Hamish wanted to touch her, to soothe her feelings.

She visibly pulled herself together. "So let's track that phone's location."

"You do know this is illegal." Shit. Of course she knew. But what a stupid git he was to bring it up.

"I am aware." She made a rolling motion with her hand.

So Hamish got down to tracking Marsh Adams's phone.

"The closest I can get is a tower near Foxhead, Massachusetts, north of Boston."

"You mean south of Boston, yes?"

"Not according to the map." He traced his finger over the area and then glanced at her again. "Definitely north."

"Huh. Marsh has a house on the Cape." Jillian leaned back in her chair, her head tilted toward the ceiling, and sighed. "So what do you suggest? We just go to Boston and wander around?"

Hamish finessed the computer keys some more. "You're thinking too linearly, love."

Her gaze flared at the endearment, then flattened. "You have a better idea?"

"Let's see if we can find any Irish pubs nearby." Hamish grinned. "Like a Venn diagram."

Jillian sat up in the chair. "So if we cross section the third circle which is the drug prescriptions along with the areas of Marsh's phone call and Irish bars, perhaps we can narrow down our search. Find the intersectionality of those three things."

Hamish's heart quickened. Finally, it felt as if they had a solid plan, and were making headway.

"I found several pubs within a five-mile radius of this town."

"That still doesn't mean he's there or she's there or they are there together," Jillian commented.

Hamish wanted to rush to Boston. Success was nearly in his grasp and finally he could apprehend Brianna Walsh. But he had to play this next part carefully, because he didn't have any jurisdiction here. He didn't have the legal authority to arrest her. And extradition to the UK was notoriously difficult. "It would be even better if we had the evidence that she stole the money."

"If she did, why didn't she access it before she disappeared?"

"Too suspicious," Hamish said. "She needed to wait until she had a new identity before she transferred cash into a bank account. Otherwise the American authorities would have caught on to her plot. We need her to admit she stole the money on recording."

"We can figure that out later." Jillian stood and stretched. "Look at how many different cell towers Marsh's phone has pinged from. According to the data we have, he has been in Portland, Vermont, New Hampshire, and Massachusetts. They could be getting ready to move again."

"So now you think he is working with her?"

She wrapped her arms around her waist in a defensive posture. "I don't know."

He could tell that admission had hurt her. She clearly wanted to believe the best in her partner. But sometimes that just wasn't possible. The final damning fact was he'd been calling his mother…and he hadn't been calling her.

"Anything else you need to share with me?" Jillian asked.

He hesitated. "Nope."

They had fallen into an easy camaraderie. One that Hamish liked far too much.

"Then I guess we're going to Boston."

"We?" He loved the sound of that.

"Yes, we."

Hamish closed the laptop with a click. "We still have to evade the Walsh brothers. They could be watching your office. And I don't think we should go back to our respective flats."

"Leave that to me." Jillian pressed the button on the intercom. "Jake. I need you."

<hr>

AFTER RAIDING THE OFFICE CLOSET—IN actuality the "closet" was a room full of clothing and accessories for recon, research trips, and the occasional undercover gig— Jill and Hamish had enough clothes to eliminate the need to visit their respective apartments.

With Jake as a decoy, they were able to avoid any tails and caught a commuter flight to Boston Logan.

Jill rented a car and they headed up the coast to the center of the geographical area that they wanted to search.

Throughout the whole process. Jillian kept hoping that the evidence would not support the truth that Marsh was helping Beatrice Winter.

But the proof was right there on the computer. On Thanksgiving day, last Thursday, Marsh's cell phone pinged off the tower north of Boston in Foxhead. The seizure drug that Beatrice needed had been purchased in the same town by three female patients. Sure, it was circumstantial, but the odds of those two events being connected were good.

The likely scenario was that Marsh was with Beatrice. Maybe…he didn't know that she was a criminal, but it wasn't looking good.

A quiet despair stole over her as she searched for logical reasons for Marsh to be hanging out with Beatrice without being in contact with Jillian. Nothing good came to mind.

"You okay?" Hamish hovered behind her.

She turned to look at him, thinking he'd been right. But if he was going to gloat, she would face it head-on.

"I'm fine."

He was closer than she'd expected, and instead of glee, he wore a look of concern. "Any man worth his salt knows that fine doesn't mean fine."

"Points for reality." Jill wanted to rest her head on his chest and just be. Instead she shifted her chin up and said, "I will be fine."

"He might have an explanation—"

"This is what you've been pushing for since you barged into my office." Jill shook her head. "Why are you backpedaling?"

He opened his mouth, paused, then tilted his head. "Oddly, I don't like to see you distressed."

Jillian wanted to laugh. Most people wouldn't be able to tell that she was upset. "What makes you think I'm distressed?"

Instead of answering, he reached for her. "Come here."

Reluctantly she let him pull her into his embrace. When his arms wrapped around her, that sense of coming home surprised her once again. "I'm fine."

"I'm not. "He hugged her closer and she buried her face in his neck. "I need a hug."

His arms felt good and she relaxed into the embrace, curling her arms around his waist. She shuddered as the tension from the past three months gutted through her.

"Fancy a drink?"

She laughed. "I thought you'd never ask."

Armed with a list of several Irish bars in the vicinity, they headed out to look for Beatrice…and Marsh.

On the third dive bar, they struck pay dirt.

"You recognize this woman?" Hamish asked. The clientele and the workers seemed more inclined to respond to a man rather than a woman.

"Who wants to know?"

"We're from Adam's Law Office." Jill couldn't stand by any longer. "She's come into an inheritance from a client of ours and we're trying to find her."

"Who is your client?" the bartender asked.

Her response was cold and absolutely sincere. "I would never betray my confidential client's identity."

The bartender a big, scary-looking dude with a sleeve of tattoos on his left arm, studied them for another moment, then gestured for them to follow. "Come on in back."

Hamish walked through the shadowy doorway first.

As soon as Jill walked through, someone grabbed her arms from behind. "What the hell?"

A guy bigger than the bartender, with a thick middle, huge biceps, and a beard a mountain man would be proud of, swung his meaty fist at Hamish's stomach.

"Ooof."

"What the hell are you doing?" she cried.

"What makes you think she's here?"

"How the hell should I know? I just go where I'm told." Jill was still pretending to be from the lawyer's office. Her stomach turned at the smell of spilled beer and fry grease. "The firm's investigator sent us here."

The big guy swung at Hamish again. Luckily he was able to dance out of the way.

Jill struggled against the other guy's hold. She didn't want to step out of her law firm character unless she had to because it appeared that they might have found Beatrice. "Let me go!"

Apparently Hamish had no such compunction about continuing to be an attorney. He swung at the brute, getting in a nice uppercut before another guy grabbed him from behind.

"I want to talk to the owner." Jill countered.

"I don't appreciate people I don't know coming into my bar and stirring shit up," the mountain man said.

He was the owner?

"How is this stirring up shit?" She had used the same pretext as in Philadelphia. "Do you know this woman? She came into some money."

"Nope." He shook his head. "We were warned about you."

Warned? So Beatrice had put an insurance plan in place. How did she even find these guys?

"Fuck this." She snapped her head back, hitting the guy holding her in the nose. The move scrambled her brain a bit, but his grip loosened as he let out a howl.

At the same time, Hamish broke free from his hold and swung at the owner's face, his fist connecting with the beefy guy's jaw with a thud. But then the guy who'd been holding him got in a shot to Hamish's jaw and he came out swinging.

Jill broke from the moaning guy's hold and whirled around. Kita's training kicked in and she performed a quick kata, taking the guy to the ground.

Hamish moved with the rough awkwardness of a brawler—it wasn't pretty but it got the job done—and managed to get a few more hooks in before he took another shot to the face.

"You have thirty seconds to get out." The owner growled. "Don't come back."

Hamish grabbed her hand and went straight out the back. They made it in ten.

____

Chapter 13

____

Hamish and Jillian stumbled into the generic hotel room. Due to an apparently awesome convention nearby, the only hotel room they could get was a small dark room with a double bed. Fortunately, Jillian was able to prepay online, and they bypassed the front desk by checking in using the digital key app on her phone. They had gotten some serious looks when they'd snuck in a side door, and he shuddered to think what would have happened if they'd had to walk through the lobby.

She'd removed her coat and shoes but was still dressed in her jeans and a loose sky blue chambray shirt that draped over her breasts and created intriguing shadows.

Hamish shrugged out of his ruined shirt, the fabric ripped, one button missing, and tossed it over the desk chair in the corner. He toed off his trainers and kicked them under the desk. He bent over to remove his socks and groaned. His whole damn body hurt.

"I still think you should go to the hospital and get checked out."

Hamish stubbornly pressed his swollen mouth together.

"I'm fine. Besides, I don't want any chance of the… altercation being reported to the police."

Jill dampened a thin washcloth in the sink with cool water. "Sit down."

He sat on the bed, legs spread, hands clasped between his knees, and closed his eyes. His eye socket throbbed with every inhale, and the rest of his body ached with soreness.

She handed him a hand towel filled with ice. "Put this on your eye."

He grumbled and pressed the ball of ice to his purpling flesh.

Jill stood between his legs and tilted his chin up so she could see his cut. She dabbed at the one-inch cut gently.

"Christ, I could use a drink," Hamish said.

"Not a good idea with a head wound." She frowned. She was so close, the lines around her mouth were bracketed, and the stress of the past few days was visible. Her position placed her breasts right in front of his face that shadow tempting him with possibilities. Impossibly, his cock thickened.

"How do you want to play this tomorrow?" she asked huskily, as if her thoughts had gone to the same place as his.

It wasn't that late. But it was a Sunday and the pharmacy was closed for the night. Life in a small town.

Hamish cleared his throat. "We're going to go to the pharmacy and see if we can narrow down which of the three women is Brianna and attempt to get her address. Assuming she didn't give a fake one, we'll stake out that address and see if we can't catch her. Hopefully the bar owner won't alert her that we were asking questions."

Hamish's eyelids drifted closed and he winced when she cleaned out the cut. He could admit to being exhausted.

They were on the right track, he could feel it. Brianna was in his sights.

Even though Jillian was the one taking care of him right now, he wanted to take care of her. "Thanks for the assist on the…" He gestured to his head.

She smiled.

"The first time you tended to me, I thought it was out of character."

She stiffened.

"Now I know that despite the tough-as-nails exterior, you hide a tender heart."

She snorted. "Fat chance."

"This is the most in-character thing you've done since I met you. You look out for everyone."

She rolled her eyes and dabbed at his cut, perhaps a little more forcefully than necessary.

"Nope." But she smiled softly as if pleased by the fact that he noticed that she was a nurturer at heart.

"Aye." Hamish prodded. "Admit it."

She ignored him. "Lean back on the pillows."

"Only if you lean with me."

She shook her head.

"You've got to be as exhausted as I am," Hamish cajoled. "It's been a long fucking day."

They had started the day in Philadelphia, in bed. He was happy that he was ending the day in Massachusetts, in bed with her again. "Come on, love."

"Fine." She tossed the damp cloth onto the end table.

Hamish scooted until his back was up against the pleated fake-leather headboard, still in his jeans and muscle vest.

Jillian hadn't removed any clothing, dressed in jeans and that chambray shirt. She sat on the edge of the bed.

Hamish put a hand to his head. "Closer, love, in case I start to feel faint."

She snorted. "Master manipulator. You're fine."

"Okay, honestly, closer because I need to hold onto you." He let the laughter fall from his face. There had been a moment, when the bouncer had held Jillian and the owner was beating the shit out of him, when he'd felt powerless. She had been struggling, her arms bound behind her back, and the guy had started to drag her away.

In that moment, a killing rage had come over Hamish. He'd wanted to obliterate the fellow. But before he could unleash his mammoth wrath, Jillian had rescued herself.

"I was afraid for you."

"The big bad NCA officer was afraid?" she teased.

"I knew eventually I would be able to break free, but I was terrified that before I could he would hurt you."

"I am perfectly able to take care of myself." As she'd proved.

"Terror isn't rational, love." He curled his arm around her shoulders and tugged her closer. Needing the contact, needing the reassurance that she was okay. The truth was he wanted more than a hug, needed that physical confirmation of her safety, a connection so pure it transcended rationality.

"Terror?" She tried to blow it off.

"I wanted to rip his fucking head off." He kissed the side of her head and inhaled the patchouli scent, triggering a primordial rush of ownership, the need to stamp his physical seal of possession a drumbeat in his veins. "For daring to harm you."

That shut her up.

"I should have known better than to walk into an unknown situation unprepared."

"There's no way we could have anticipated that attack."

"Brianna is a master at convincing people to do what she wants." Hamish squeezed her tighter. "I forgot and let down my guard."

His heart had nearly stopped when the bouncer had grabbed her.

"I'm okay." She attempted to calm him, stroking her hand down in his naked biceps. "You're okay…sort of."

His body responded to her soft stroke, his cock throbbing in time to the light touch, and he groaned.

"If you aren't going to go to the hospital, I'll need to check on you every few hours."

"I'm at your disposal."

"That sounds rather…provocative."

"Use me at your will." He didn't have many close friends. And it had been a while since he'd had a lover. But he could get used to this. He and Charlie had been competitive. Charlie had been the jock, while Hamish had been the nerd.

But being a nerd had some benefits.

He'd studied female anatomy.

Just like cybercrime, where one small piece of intelligence could send an investigation into another level, a woman's body was similar. He wanted to find her hidden erotic spots and bring her pleasure.

Hamish took her hand in his and stroked his fingers over the calluses he'd noticed the other day.

Now he realized they came from knitting. He stroked her hands with long slow pressure from his thumbs.

She moaned and his cock thickened again.

"That feels really good," she breathed against his neck. "How did you know?"

"I grew up on a sheep farm. My mam knits sweaters to sell during the winters." He continued to rub as she snuggled closer. "It can be hard on the hands."

She must knit a lot.

"You have strong hands." He raised her palm to his mouth and kissed the center softly.

She sighed and he kissed her again, this time caressing her skin with the tip of his tongue. Jillian lay on his chest, her chin tilted up and her gaze caught on his.

She curled her fingers around his neck and brought his mouth to hers.

Hamish's heart constricted.

The moment felt significant.

She kissed him gently.

"Harder, love."

"I'm trying not to hurt your mouth." She feathered her fingertips over his swollen mouth.

"It will hurt more if you don't give me a proper kiss."

Hamish skimmed his fingers along her ribcage, lifting the soft chambray shirt so he could stroke her skin.

She arched into his touch.

He threaded his fingers through hers and rolled them so that he lay between her legs.

As her head hit the pillow, she winced.

"What's wrong?"

"Ah, I'm a bit sore from the head butt."

He rolled them again so they lay on their sides facing each other. "You're a bad ass." He brushed the loose strands of hair from her cheek.

"Yeah, I'll have to thank Kita." She joked.

"Me too." He pressed a kiss to her forehead. "You hurt anywhere else?"

He wanted to take care of her. Wanted to soothe away every hurt and ache and wrap her up in a cocoon of safety.

She started to shake her head.

"Think about it before you answer."

Jillian stared into his eyes, her chameleon gaze softening to the mottled gray of a Spring sky near his hometown. Mysterious and compelling at the same time. "I really am good."

She trailed her fingers over his chest and gently brushed below his sternum. Now it was Hamish's turn to wince.

"Does it hurt?"

"I'll get over it." He brushed off her concern. Because they were out of that back room and safe and they had a solid lead on Brianna. Life was good.

She brushed a kiss over his throbbing cheekbone. "Where's your ice?"

She was doing it again, tending to him.

Jillian softly, slowly pressed her mouth to his, the touch light and tender. Hamish closed his eyes, gave himself over to her caress as he opened for the sensual assault.

He skimmed his fingers over the dip in her chambray top stroking the soft flesh between her breasts as she kissed her way down the bumps and bruises of his face and shoulders. He leaned closer and inhaled her scent, the musky aroma calming him.

Hamish slowly unbuttoned her shirt, wincing at the stiffness in his cracked knuckles. When he got to the button of her jeans, the scraped skin brushed against her belly.

"Your hands," she murmured. "Let me."

She quickly unbuttoned her jeans, pulled down the zipper, and wiggled out of them.

Hamish's breath backed up in his throat at the gift she was giving him.

He'd really only wanted to hold her and feel her in his arms.

But as she held his gaze and let the blouse drop from her shoulders to reveal a lacy bra in a pristine white, his brain shifted to more carnal thoughts.

The sheer lace didn't conceal the hard points of her nipples, and he couldn't wait to sample her. He bent his head to worship her, closing his lips over the lace, tonguing the hard berry.

She moaned and gripped his head, pulling him closer.

JILLIAN'S ACHES slipped away as Hamish licked his way over the mounds of her breasts. Then he sucked her nipple, zapping her with a direct line to her sex. He cupped her breasts in his hands. He should be resting but she couldn't bring herself to stop him.

His cock throbbed hard and insistent against the soft skin of her belly.

She scraped her fingers through his hair arching her back and pushing her breast into his kiss.

She cupped him through his jeans, the hot length pulsing against her palm. "Happy to see me?"

He stopped kissing her. "You know it, love." He pressed a line of kisses down the center of her stomach, stopping to pay close attention to her belly button, the soft hair of his beard a sensual caress, while his fingers traced the line of her panties. Her belly contracted at the soft touch.

Jillian moaned, then pushed her hands inside his underwear and curved her palm around his silky hard erection.

She pumped once, twice, savoring the thick length of him. Her core clenched, craving him inside her.

She wanted him pressing her into the soft mattress of

the bed, covering her with his body. But her head still hurt so that would have to wait for another time.

His eyes were closed, his lashes dark against the bruised skin of his cheekbone, and her heart stumbled. He'd taken quite the beating and she couldn't bear to hurt him. "Maybe we should stop. I don't want to hurt you."

"Stop? Are you daft?" He lifted his head from his very thorough exploration of her body.

She snorted. "That's not very complimentary."

"You're brilliant and half-starkers and I'm clearly up for the job." He rolled onto his back releasing her, and his erection rose from the open V of his jeans. "Why would we stop?"

"You're pretty beat up."

"Then make me feel better." He grinned at her, his swollen bottom lip slightly cockeyed.

"You're sure?"

He pushed his jeans to his ankles and lifted his hips to shove them off to the end of the bed. He lifted his hand showing off the condom packet between two fingers.

"I guess you're sure." Since he was on his back, she lifted up and straddled him.

"Ho now, what's this." He cupped her ass and rubbed his thumbs over her hip bones then slid them down until he stroked her clit. "These need to come off."

All her blood rushed south and she could only nod. *God, don't stop that.*

Jill skimmed her panties off while Hamish dispensed with her bra.

When she was above him on all fours, she began to lift the tank undershirt up from his rippled abs. He must not spend all his time at the keyboard.

But he grimaced. "Let's just leave that where it is, shall we?"

Jill sat back on her knees, her butt on the back of his thighs. She watched his slightly darker fingers slide through her blond curls to play with her clit. Jill's heart beat accelerated, thumping against her breastbone with a mix of anticipation and wonder.

Desire blasted through her with each sensuous caress.

She wrapped her hands around his erection, the dark skin and engorged head leaked with the evidence of his arousal. She swiped her thumb over the head and spread the liquid so she could pump his cock in steady strokes.

He penetrated her with one finger, then two, rubbing her g-spot and hitting every erogenous nerve inside her. He was gentle, so deliberate and cautious, stoking her arousal with every tender glide of his fingers. The slow ascent to pleasure was an effortless climb until she soared off the cliff. Her hands tightened on his cock as she threw her head back and let the orgasm, the pleasure cascade through her. She shivered and shook as the aftershocks rolled over her in waves. Hamish continued to stroke and comfort as she flowed over his fingers.

"Put the rubber on, love." He cupped her breasts, tugging on her nipples with his rough fingers as she rolled the condom over his erection.

"Let me do the work." *Let me give you pleasure. Let me give you peace.* That's what she wanted to say. Instead she sheathed him quickly.

Jillian lifted up on her knees and positioned her sex over his erection.

He raised his hips, rubbing the head along her swollen sex. She sank down on him slowly, reveling in his invasion as he penetrated her with intoxicating slowness until he was seated fully inside her.

He groaned.

"Are you hurt?"

"Nothing that can't be fixed." Hamish smiled. "Move, love."

She'd promised to do the work, so Jillian began to move, rising and falling on his cock, holding onto his biceps as she used her thigh muscles to control their rhythm.

"Come here." He beckoned with a crook of his finger and Jillian bent over.

Hamish ran his hands up her back stroking her bare skin and tracing the bumps of her spine, the trail of his fingers causing more shivers.

Jillian was careful not to lean on his chest and stomach as she rode him slowly.

He stared up at her, his navy eyes dark and intense, watching as she controlled the pace of their joining. His cock swelled inside her, growing bigger, and his hips punched up, becoming more insistent.

The deep shove hit her g-spot and she moaned again.

Hamish's hands went to her hips, increasing the pace as he thrust faster and faster. Her breath quickened as he watched her as if she were a puzzle he wanted to solve. His hands roamed up to her breasts and squeezed.

Her breath caught as the sharp pinch of his fingers caused her womb to contract again.

"Like that?"

"I'm supposed to be doing the work."

"It's not work if you're having fun."

His little joke surprised her and she laughed. Laughed!

His muscles strained as his pace quickened and his cock

grew thicker inside her. The bump of his pubic bone against her clit threw her over again.

Jillian cried out as her orgasm slammed into her.

Hamish groaned and arched beneath her. His cock jerked inside her in hard insistent pumps as he flew into the abyss with her.

Jillian collapsed next to him, rolling so she didn't crush his already battered body. But she collapsed with a smile on her face. He curled his arm around her shoulders, and she nestled into the curve of his neck.

***

HAMISH'S BODY pulsed with aftershocks. They'd have to move soon, clean up. But right now he savored the intimacy of their positions. She was so damn giving, so willing to take care of everyone, even in the aftermath of an explosive orgasm she'd carefully disentangled so that she didn't hurt him.

His brain was blotto; endorphins from really excellent sex had him addled and not thinking clearly. Which is why he blurted out the question that had been festering at the back of his mind for a while. "What really happened with your witness?"

She blinked. Stopped smiling. "He died."

"Nope." He mimicked her earlier comment. "Tell me."

"It's classified."

"Ha. So I was right," Hamish crowed. "Tell me."

"Hypothetically, an informant against the mob has a much greater chance of being killed in WitSec than other witnesses."

That didn't explain what really happened, but he waited patiently.

"Hypothetically a situation could be set up to make it look like he'd been killed."

"But what I don't understand is why, hypothetically of course, someone would torpedo their career in order to make that scenario believable."

All the hypothetically was getting old. "I was in love with him."

That shut him up.

Yes, the morals and ethics queen had broken all sorts of rules.

"You…sacrificed your career so that he could live."

When you put it like that.

"Yes," she said softly.

Hamish was silent for a moment, trailing his finger over her shoulder and down her arm. She arched into him, needing the comfort of his touch.

"That's…."

"Crazy. Insane." Nothing she hadn't heard before.

"Unbelievably heroic."

Her heart melted. Even Marsh and Dee had thought she was crazy. But at the time, she couldn't bear to think of a world without Dominic in it.

He pressed another kiss to the side of her head.

"The hardest part was dealing with the fallout." All the people who thought she'd been so enthralled that she'd put her protectee's life in jeopardy. "People who were close to me believed I'd put everyone, including Dominic, in danger."

"But you went on to start Adams-Larsen."

"Sure. But my father still doesn't speak to me."

"Your da?"

She shrugged as if it still didn't hurt immensely. They'd

been a pair for a long time. Ever since her mother left when Jill had been a kid.

"I'm over it." *Mostly.*

And yes, she had abandonment issues. How could she not? But she'd thought she was over them until Marsh had ghosted her over the past three months.

"What about your mam?"

"She left when I was a little kid."

"How could she leave you?"

Wasn't that sweet. "She never really wanted me. My mother got pregnant to try and use my cells to save my brother."

"You have a brother?"

"No. He died before I was born. Cancer."

Seven words pretty much summed up her life. Everything that had happened in her life was about her brother.

She'd been trying to atone since she was born. So she really did understand his need to avenge his brother.

He was silent for a few moments. "What are the beanies for?"

Yes, even her hobby was about atonement. "For children undergoing chemo. To keep their heads warm."

"You're an extraordinary woman, love."

Yeah. So extraordinary that everyone left.

He squeezed her close as if he'd heard her thoughts. "You have your partner."

Marsh had left the agency with her and they'd started Adams-Larsen. She'd been given a severance with sealed terms so no one would ever learn of her role in saving Dominic. Everyone would always believe that she'd be negligent on the job. "He's always been my biggest supporter."

So where she found herself now hurt doubly bad. She wanted to have faith in Marsh. She did. But the circumstantial evidence pointed to him being with Beatrice.

"What does Adams-Larsen really do?"

The languid post-sex glow shattered. Sharing about Dominic was a big step but telling him about ALIAS?

He sighed. "Forget I asked."

But she couldn't forget. And truly she owed him an explanation. They had made Brianna Walsh aka Beatrice Winter disappear. She'd been trying to do the right thing but instead she had helped a criminal escape justice.

Jill inhaled, the scent of sex filling the room. Passion, desire, love competed with remorse. She didn't want to be sorry, she wanted to be happy, fulfilled.

Her heart thudded and her palms went damp. Maybe he didn't realize what a watershed moment this was but she understood that she trusted him. On a deep visceral level she knew that he would safeguard her admission and protect her secret.

"We relocate people who are in danger but don't qualify for government protection."

"How hard was that?" he teased.

"Pretty damn." She snuggled into his embrace. "I've never told anyone who didn't work for me what we actually do."

He was silent, absorbing her confession. "So why did you help Brianna?"

"My old boss asked for a favor," Jill said. "Said there was a leak in their office regarding that case and she was concerned for the client's safety."

Which the more she thought about it, the more she wondered what had been going through Dee's mind when she asked.

"Have you done many favors for her?"

"No. This was the first." Jill said, "She's referred a few clients to us but we've never placed a federal witness before."

"I've only got one more question."

She tensed, wondering how much more she could reveal. She felt flayed open and raw. Exposed by the baring of her soul. But she owed him an answer.

"Go ahead."

Hamish yawned widely, his jaw cracking audibly in the hushed hotel room. "If you loved him, why didn't you go with him?"

"He didn't ask." There had been moments where she had wanted him to, but Jill had spent her whole life working toward being a marshal just like her dad, and Dominic had known that. He'd known about her dreams. Except she'd ended up giving up her dreams for him anyway.

Hamish's eyes drifted closed. "I would have asked." His soft snore filled the room. She was going to have to wake him up periodically. Just because they didn't go to the hospital, she was still going to follow concussion protocol and check him every few hours.

His simple exhale caused a pang in her chest.

He brought up a good point. Dom hadn't even asked. And she hadn't pushed him. She could have made the request but growing up her father's love had been conditional. And his exacting standards had been hard to maintain. But she'd tried. The truth was she'd sacrificed her career for love yes, but also for freedom. Because now she was her own boss.

And she fucking loved it.

Most of the time.

"Don't fall asleep yet. It's time for your concussion check."

He exhaled softly and she poked him. "Hamish, I need to confirm you are up to snuff." She stroked her palms over his muscled chest. The sheet covering his lower half tented.

He raised his arms over his head and stretched. "I'm up to something."

"Smart ass."

"Does that count as passing?"

"How are you feeling?"

"I think I'm feeling faint." His grin widened. "All my blood has vacated my brain."

She persisted, even though she was pretty sure he was fine. "Who's the vice president?"

"Do we have to do this?" he groaned.

"Yes." She tapped him on his bare chest. "Vice President?"

"I haven't the foggiest, love," he grinned at her, eyes twinkling. "But the Queen is still the Queen. Perhaps you can help me with my…problem."

"Fine." She pressed him onto his back and straddled his hips. "Lie back and think of England."

Chapter 14

Getting the information from the pharmacy was a
challenge.

The process took time they didn't have. All three women
were relatively the same age and Brianna could pass for any
of them.

They ruled out one because of her location, a larger
home on the ocean that she had lived in for ten years.

The final two women were the same age, Brigid Pilsen
and Annabella Streeter.

Hamish's heart quickened. "It's Brigid."

"What makes you say that?"

"That was her grandmother's name."

"Okay, we'll check that one out first."

They staked out Brigid Pilsen's address. It was a typical
New England house chopped up with a separate entrance to
add an in-law apartment or a small rental unit for additional
income. Besides the front door with the peeling red paint,
there was another entrance on the back side that fed into an
alley. After watching for about an hour, Brianna made an
appearance.

"We've got her." The woman who had hurt his brother was finally in his grasp.

She tromped down the set of half stairs in tennis shoes, a pair of tight cropped jeans, and an even tighter T-shirt with the name of the bar emblazoned across her ample chest. That explained why the owner and his goons had gone after them. She must work there. She dumped a bag of trash in the can and then headed back inside.

"This is it."

"I have a confession." Hamish took a deep breath. She was going to be pissed. And he couldn't blame her. "I don't have extradition papers."

Jillian whipped her head around.

"Are you fucking kidding me?" she whispered back. "Can you get your boss on the phone and get some quick?"

Hamish shook his head. "This isn't actually a sanctioned visit."

"What did you think you were going to do once we found her?"

"I wasn't really counting on finding her. But it was my last hope." Hamish just looked at her. "And that maybe she would confess to stealing the money, and then she would have violated her agreement with the government."

She hesitated.

Hamish's stomach flipped. "Can we hold her until we can find the money or get her to confess?"

"We'll take her back to the hotel," Jill caved. "We'll go from there."

"Thank you." He shifted in the front seat of the car and clasped her face in his hands. He pressed a soft, reverent kiss to her lips.

"Don't thank me yet." Jillian pulled away from his kiss, clearly uncomfortable with the thanks. "Is she dangerous?"

"Physically? I don't believe so." Hamish knew Brianna. "She doesn't touch guns. But she could have a knife."

"How do you want to handle this?" Jill reached behind the seat and pulled out a small pistol.

"Where did that come from?" It was the first Hamish had seen of it.

"We are apprehending a criminal. What else would I bring?" She efficiently checked the weapon and pulled the slide in preparation for using it. Then she tucked the weapon into a small holster clipped at her waist on her right hip.

"Roger that." Hamish hesitated. "We've got to play this so that she believes she can turn you."

Jillian nodded.

"How good at improvising are you?"

"I'll make it work."

"Just…go along with whatever I say." Hamish squeezed her bicep. "Don't believe any of it."

"Okay." She blinked.

"We could wait until she leaves for work." But it was midmorning. Her workday might not start for hours, and in the meantime the owner of the bar could warn her.

"We know where she is right now. It's time," Jillian said.

He wasn't even sure why he was hesitating, but he was unsettled.

"No sign of Marsh." He could hear the relief in her voice. It seemed impossible that her partner wasn't involved with Brianna. He'd come to know her in the past few days and knew that Marsh's defection would hurt her, but he said it anyway. "He could be inside."

Her eyes darkened for a moment and then she nodded sharply. "I'll take the back entrance. You take the front."

"Let's do it."

They eased out of the car simultaneously, their doors closing with a quiet thunk.

"Wait until I'm in position before you go up the stairs. I'll cover the back entrance in case she tries to bolt when she sees you." Then Jillian marched toward the rear entrance.

The apartment itself was tiny. Almost shotgun style from one entrance to the other. Hamish had a feeling when the front door was open, he'd be able to see all the way to the back exit.

He patted his jacket pocket with the zip ties. This was the tricky part. He had no jurisdiction here. His boss would be furious. Jillian wasn't very happy with him either.

Maybe he should be sorry he bugged her office, but he wasn't. And because of that intel, he had begun tracing the email account that her guy Viktor had found. Brianna had taken several trips to the Dominican Republic while she worked for America's Recovery Centers. The Caribbean was a banking haven. With a little more time, he might have been able to find the money.

He had hacked into Jill's email and sent Kita Kim the information about Brianna's email along with a note to follow it for a money trail. Since he couldn't be in two places at once and he would never want Jill to attempt to apprehend Brianna on her own, he had to let go of his grip on the information.

Once Jillian was in place, he walked up to the door confidently. The lights were on in the small apartment and Hamish could see Brianna's shadow in the bedroom. She was shouting over her shoulder at someone out of sight in the kitchen.

So there were two of them.

JILLIAN CREPT up the back steps, her heart in her throat. She prayed Marsh wasn't here. She could see all the way through the apartment and Hamish was at the front door.

Apprehension fizzed through her bloodstream. Executing a takedown with only two agents was risky, but necessary in this case.

ALIAS had let Beatrice loose on the world to possibly hurt more people. Because the reality was women like Beatrice never changed.

She was a user.

And morally bankrupt.

Jill's mission in life was to protect the innocent. But doing this for Hamish could damage ALIAS's reputation beyond repair.

She was torn between her employees and clients, and Hamish's wishes. She'd been born to serve the greater good and her brother had died anyway. Her whole life she'd atoned for that by living in service to others and protecting the weak. But now she had the overwhelming urge to protect Hamish. Somehow in the past few days, he'd become important.

There was someone at the other end of the alley and they were eyeing her, likely wondering what she was doing hovering outside the door.

Rotting food and piss overwhelmed the air.

Fuck it. Illegal entry was the least of their problems. She reached out to see if the door was open, and miraculously the knob turned in her hand. She slipped inside the kitchen while Hamish was knocking on the front door. She was so intent on Hamish, she missed the figure in the corner.

"Jill?" Marsh stood in the kitchen dressed in jeans and a plain white T-shirt, his hair shaggy, and his face haggard and unshaven.

Her heart dropped. He was with Beatrice. And he hadn't called her in weeks.

"What the hell are you doing here?" He glanced frantically toward the open bedroom door.

He grabbed her arm and pulled her toward him.

Hamish was still banging on the front door.

"Can you get the front door, babe?" Marsh shoved Jill behind him. "I don't want the eggs to burn."

"You have to get out of here," he said desperately. "Before she sees you."

Jill hadn't said a word. Marsh's betrayal stabbed her in the chest like a hot poker.

"Hold yer horses." Beatrice stomped to the front door and yanked it open.

Jill shoved Marsh out of the way and went to back up Hamish. She would deal with Marsh later.

"What do you want?" Beatrice sneered at Hamish.

"I want you to pay for your crimes."

"You can't touch me here, Officer Ballard." Her tone was insolent. "You look like you got your ass kicked."

Hamish saw Jill and nodded. "We got her."

Beatrice whirled around. She hadn't heard Jill, and now Marsh, approach from behind.

"Ms. Larsen." Beatrice morphed before Jill's eyes. "This horrible man just burst into my apartment." But a frown crimped her face for a minute and Jill saw the evil beneath. "Although what are you doing here? I thought you weren't supposed to have any contact with me."

Jill just looked at her and then Marsh.

"Who is this guy?" Marsh asked from behind her.

This whole thing was a cluster fuck. "Beatrice, Marsh, go sit on the sofa."

"Babe, are you going to let her talk to me that way?" Beatrice had propped her fists on her hips.

"Jillian and her friend were just leaving," Marsh said.

"I don't think so." Jill backed up two steps and shifted so she could see everyone in her sights and she pulled her gun from its holster. "Go sit on the sofa."

"I'm sure this is all just a misunderstanding," Marsh said calmly.

"Nope."

Marsh was slow to move, his hand in his pocket.

"Hands out of your pockets." Jill waved them toward the sofa. "Where I can see them."

"What is it that you think you're going to do here?" Beatrice said cockily from the sofa. She was completely relaxed.

"So this is him then?" Hamish identified Marsh.

"Jill, who is this guy?" Marsh's tone was oddly territorial.

"Officer Hamish Ballard meet Marshall Adams," Jill said tiredly. The past few months pressed in on her. All that worry, all that heartache, and Marsh had been with Beatrice Winter the whole time.

"You okay, love?"

A warmth spread in her chest. Hamish had been chasing Beatrice forever. And yet, he'd noticed she was upset and checked in on her.

"I will be."

Marsh looked…confused. "You guys need to go. We don't want you here."

Jill discreetly put her hand inside her peacoat and pressed record on her phone. "What did you do with the money, Beatrice?"

For just a moment, Beatrice smirked. "I have no idea

what you're talking about. My next paycheck isn't until the end of the week."

"I bet if we search your apartment, we will find drugs." Hamish poked around.

"What are you talking about?" Marsh's gaze shot from Jill to Beatrice and back again.

"Your girlfriend here likes to push drugs." Jill tossed Hamish a pair of vinyl gloves.

"You're actually *selling* drugs?" Marsh shook his head as if in disbelief.

Beatrice reached for his hand and held between her two palms like she was praying. "Don't listen to a word they say."

"What happened to your accent, *Brianna?*" Jill asked.

"Who's Brianna?" Marsh asked.

"You're done, Brianna." Jill wanted to kick something or someone. Jury was out on whether she'd go for Beatrice or Marsh first. "Or Beatrice, or Brigid, or whatever you're calling yourself now."

"Bugger off."

Marsh pulled his hand from Beatrice's clasp.

Hamish prowled the apartment, searching for any indication that Beatrice was up to her old ways, and sure enough there was a bag taped inside the toilet bowl. "Pretty predictable, Brianna. You're getting sloppy."

Marsh rubbed his palms over his thighs. "Can someone please explain what is going on?"

"Maybe you should have listened to your messages, partner." Jill asked the woman again, "What did you do with the money?"

"I don't know what you're talking about."

"Specifically the money you stole from the America's

Recovery Centers." Jill glanced around the shabby apartment. "You certainly aren't using it here."

Marsh interjected. "The executives stole the money."

"We're living frugally until Marsh's inheritance comes through," Beatrice said defiantly. "That isn't a crime."

Marsh's inheritance? Marsh already had his money. They'd used his trust fund and Jill's 401K to get ALIAS off the ground. That didn't make any sense.

"So move along."

They weren't going to get anywhere with this bitch. Maybe she'd open up once she was in custody.

"Okay, let's take them in," Jill said calmly.

"Take *us* in?" Marsh frowned.

"Sounds good. After all, I really need Brianna now." Hamish bluffed. "I found the money."

Jill jerked. What?

Beatrice snorted. "What money?" she said slyly.

"Right then. You won't mind if I help myself."

"Good luck with that." Beatrice rolled her eyes.

"You know I work cybercrimes." Hamish said, "I don't need luck. I just need secure access and your password… which I know is Brigid1935."

Beatrice jolted. "You can't get in without me."

"Good thing I also know how to create fake extradition orders." Hamish crossed his arms. "You're coming with me."

Jill knew he was lying and still she had a moment of doubt.

"Mr. Goody Goody?" she said derisively. "You are going to steal money from someone?"

"Yeah well, my career is fucked. My brother is dead." His voice broke. "And if I can't make you pay, then I'm going to take the only thing you care about."

"What?!" Jill shouted. The fierce conviction in his voice sent shiver of apprehension through her. What if she'd misjudged him? "You can't do that."

Beatrice blinked. Narrowed her gaze at Hamish.

"I believe I can." He grinned. One Jill had never seen before, nearing evil. "Fuck you, Brianna."

"I thought we were together on this." Jill pretended to ignore Beatrice and plead with Hamish. "I trusted you."

"You're in the business of lies." Hamish's voice was cold, hard. "You should never have trusted me."

He strode toward Beatrice, zip ties dangling from his fist.

"I have the gun." Jill shot back.

"And you're not going to use it," Hamish said. "Too many pesky rules."

Jill could see her literally switch gears. Beatrice began to toss out bribes to Jill. "You're right. I have the money." She ignored Hamish and appealed to Jill. "I'm willing to share."

Jill glared at Hamish, stringing Beatrice along, pretending to think about it. "I'm listening." She couldn't bear to lie but she wanted to see where Beatrice was going with this.

Beatrice studied her assessing whether she was truthful or not and Jill knew she needed to sell this.

She shifted the gun to point at Hamish. "Pretty sure my reputation isn't lily white. Step away from Ms. Winter or I may have to shoot you."

Hamish stopped dead. And Jill verbally prodded Beatrice. "You embezzled the money from the rehab centers."

"Aye." Now that her identity was out, Beatrice stopped hiding her accent. "Stupid gits."

"Why?"

"The British government found most of my off shore

accounts. I was broke!" She grumbled. "I needed a new nest egg."

"Why not just get the money that was still there?"

"I needed a new passport to get the money. I knew the British government would be monitoring the one they gave me, so I couldn't use Beatrice. I needed a completely new identity." Beatrice shrugged. "I had to lie low for a while."

"Lie low by taking money from an illegal operation and then turning them in?" Hamish said incredulously.

"Well, the itch to fuck with them just wouldn't go away…you can never have too much." She gloated.

"Adams-Larsen gave you a new identity. Why not use it?"

"Marsh followed me." Beatrice sighed dramatically. "It was *so* romantic. And I had a…separate issue."

Separate issue? Jill decided to switch tactics. She'd come back to that comment later.

"Why did you really turn your family in?" Jill asked as if the answer didn't really interest her.

"Men." Beatrice huffed in exasperation. "They don't respect a strong woman," she said trying to appeal to Jillian's sense of sisterhood.

"You're right." Jill tossed a glance at Marsh. "We are underappreciated."

Beatrice thought she was getting somewhere. Jillian didn't look at Hamish, didn't want to give away that she was playing Beatrice. And Jill let her dig the hole deeper.

"Exactly," Beatrice said with satisfaction. "We're smarter than all of them put together."

"So it was pure revenge?" Jill asked curiously.

"I was running the whole damn business." Beatrice shook her head, her blond curls swaying. "But I showed them."

"What now?" Jill asked.

"Well, since Officer Ballard doesn't have paperwork," Beatrice smiled slyly. "Perhaps we can work out a deal. Just between us girls. I prefer negotiating with women anyway."

"What about Marsh?" Jill didn't look at her partner.

"Means to an end. I needed to stay off radar until it was safe to go to Turks and Caicos and get my money." Beatrice rolled her eyes. "Men are so gullible."

"Hey!" Marsh said.

"Sorry, darling."

"You were using me?" He sounded calculating rather than upset.

"See. Gullible."

"I know what you mean," Jill said. "So is that why you targeted Marsh on that first day?"

"Among other reasons." Now Beatrice seemed to be in a sharing mood. "I had your old boss brief me on the two of you. But I figured from the outset that he would be my best bet."

"Show a man your tits and they're slaves to sex." Jill laughed.

"Quite right." Beatrice smiled like the Cheshire cat. "When we get away from here, you and I can work out a deal."

She was very convincing. Jill had a better understanding of how she had manipulated people. She appealed to their sense of superiority, making them feel like they were smarter than everyone else in the room. Dummies.

"Why did you sell drugs to the patients?" Hamish asked.

"I didn't sell drugs to patients." Beatrice chuckled. "However, I may have put them in touch with people who could help them out."

"Wasn't that against the terms of your court agreement?" Hamish asked.

Beatrice ignored him, bragging to Jill. "Since I was underage when I was caught, they gave me community service. So dumb. They just gave me a new avenue to find customers. But I never *sold* drugs again. That scared straight weekend in youth detention center was enough for me. I am never going to prison."

Jillian hated this woman. Hated her with the fire of a thousand suns. "You never sold drugs again?"

"I never *sold* them again."

"What about the drugs in this baggie?" Hamish wagged the baggie full of pills.

"*Gifts* for a friend." Who then was going to sell them. She was couching her behavior on a technicality.

"I may have given away a freebie once." She laughed, her blue eyes sparkling. On the outside she appeared as an attractive fortyish woman but the rot in her soul came through. "As a matter of fact, I may have gifted them to someone you know. Oh, excuse me, someone you used to know."

You fucking bitch. Jill's hands gripped her weapon so tight, her knuckles were white. The urge to shoot her was a physical compulsion but she beat it back. They needed this damn confession.

She couldn't look at Hamish. Couldn't bear to see pain on his face.

"Why?" He burst out. "You offered my brother drugs. More than once."

"Ah yes. Charlie Ballard. Such a fabulous rugby player for Scotland. I sure did Ireland a solid when he was gone."

"But why?"

"Quid pro quo for a…friend, part of the Russians you

were investigating. Apparently you were getting a little too close to their hacker and they wanted you distracted."

Her words were going to gut him.

She had targeted Charlie because he was related to Hamish. To disrupt his investigation.

"Besides, addicts are a waste on society. All they do is take, take, take. Overdoses are inevitable."

"He was getting better," Hamish ground out.

"Tsk, tsk, Officer Ballard. He was an addict. He was already doomed."

"You are not responsible for her actions," Jill said fiercely, no longer willing to humor Beatrice.

Jill shifted her weapon and trained it securely on Beatrice and Marsh. Jill had enough recorded that they could take Beatrice in. Her confession was enough to put her away here, even if she never made it back to the UK. "Okay. Sharing time is over."

"But I thought we had a deal." Beatrice widened her gaze.

"I'm reneging," Jill said.

"You cow." Beatrice shifted on the sofa, clearly searching for a way out or what to use as a weapon.

"I'm an excellent markswoman," Jill said to Beatrice. "I excel at the moving target drill and I haven't gotten in my practice for this month. So don't try it."

Beatrice relaxed back against the ugly sofa.

"Or better yet, please do try it." Jill grinned. And it wasn't nice. "I need some work on isolating specific limbs."

———————————

Chapter 15

———————————

A knock on the door interrupted the tense moment.
Who the fuck was here now?

An older woman, dark brown hair pulled back into a tight bun, similar to the style Jillian wore her hair, and cargo pants and a tight black top, opened the door and walked in as if she owned the place.

"Good work, Jill." She nodded tightly. "I'll take her from here."

What now?

"Ms. Womack!" Brianna jumped to her feet.

"What are you doing here?" Jillian kept her weapon trained on Brianna but the frown on her face said a lot.

Had Jillian notified her old boss that they were closing in on Brianna?

"How did you get here so fast?" That was from Marsh Adams.

Fast? Something peculiar was happening here but Hamish kept his mouth shut.

He should focus on what was happening in this shitty

little apartment but his anguish was like a river of shame flowing through him. Brianna had just devastated him.

Before he'd just thought that his inattention to his brother was to blame for him not seeing that Charlie was struggling. But now he knew the truth. His brother had been targeted because of Hamish's job.

"I'm going to make sure you never see the light of day," he vowed.

"You have no jurisdiction here, Officer Ballard," Deanna Womack said crisply.

Certain things weren't adding up. What was she doing here? And how did she know his name? Had Jillian told Womack he was here when she'd met with the woman?

Had she been stringing him along this whole time?

"You need to go back to your own country." Deanna Womack whipped out flex cuffs and clipped Brianna Walsh's wrists together. "I'll take care of this one."

"I'll go with you," Jill piped up.

"No need." Womack tugged Brianna toward the front door. "I've got her."

Beatrice smiled. She didn't appear upset at all.

Hamish pulled himself out of his pit of grief. His brother was dead. He couldn't change that, and something weird was going on right now.

"What about Marsh?" Jillian asked.

"Technically he didn't do anything illegal." Deanna shrugged. "He's free to go."

Marsh Adams bristled. "Seriously?"

Jillian shot him such a look of disdain it was a wonder that the man didn't crumble on the spot. "I'll go with you," she repeated to Deanna.

"Really, not necessary."

"I'm not letting anything interfere with bringing her to justice." Jill tucked her weapon into the holster at her side.

"I'd prefer to come as well." Something was totally off about this whole fucking thing. The level of panic rising inside Hamish threw him off. But he trusted his gut. And something was terribly, terribly wrong.

"Dee's right. You have no jurisdiction here." She reached up and kissed his cheek. She handed him her phone. She was trying to impart some wisdom with her gaze. But Hamish had no fucking clue what was going on.

"The digital room key is in the app so you can get your stuff."

They'd have to discuss the lack of security on a digital key later. But Hamish just nodded. "Quite right. I'll wait for you."

"Don't bother." Jillian shook her head. "I have plenty of burners. It's not important."

"But—"

"No regrets." She smiled wistfully. "I know you'll do the right thing."

She flicked at glance at her partner but didn't say a word.

He watched her get into the car with Marshal Womack and the woman he'd hated. Something was off but he wasn't putting it all together.

"Can I get a ride?" Marsh Adams followed him out the door.

Hamish wanted to say no. Actually he wanted to punch the bloke, but he restrained himself. "Fine."

Something made Hamish decide to follow the sporty red car with Jillian inside.

He thought he'd feel more triumphant. But as he stared

at the back of the car with Brianna and Jillian in it, he realized that nothing was going to bring his brother back.

Hamish was more worried about Jillian and how she was handling her partner's betrayal.

"What's the deal with you and my partner?" Marsh Adams asked. Curious. He didn't ask about Brianna or why they were after her. He wanted to know about Jillian.

"None of your business." Hamish was feeling surly. He didn't like that Jillian had basically told him not to let the door hit him in the arse.

"Something is wrong," Marsh said.

"You're a twat. That's what's wrong," Hamish snarled. "You didn't contact her for months."

"I was undercover."

"Say what?"

"I was trying to get a location on the money."

"So you sold out your partner?"

"No. I was working for Deanna."

The car in front of them took an unexpected turn. Hamish wasn't used to driving on the right side of the road. The unfamiliar placement of the steering wheel and the extra concentration to stay in the proper lane slowed him down.

"Are you saying that Deanna Womack knew where you were all along?"

"Sure. I filed weekly reports with her."

"Then why didn't you contact Jillian?"

"Because Dee made that a condition of the op. I had to go completely dark."

"She's been worried sick about you." She compromised herself to find her partner. And another thought occurred to Hamish. "So if Deanna Womack knew where you were, why'd she show up just now?"

The only things that had changed were Hamish had revealed her password and Brianna had confessed that she had the money. "Was your apartment bugged?"

"No. I sent Dee an SOS when you and Jill arrived."

But that was only about forty-five minutes ago. "You may be wrong about that bugging, mate." Or had Deanna followed Jill and Hamish? Shite. "Something is not adding up here."

Jillian had been trying to tell him something when she'd handed him the phone. There was a moment. He had to trust Marsh right here. "Can I trust you?"

"About as much as I can trust you."

He was perfectly trustworthy.

He reached into his pocket and pulled out the phone she'd given him. "Check that. There's something on there that she wanted me to have."

Marsh was quiet as he studied the phone. "There's a recording."

Marsh pressed play. They listened in silence. Jillian had captured everything he needed to convince his boss to extradite Brianna Walsh back to the UK.

Hamish should be jubilant. But right now all he could think about was Jillian.

That crazy woman had put herself in the car with the woman responsible for his brother's death and her former boss, who she clearly didn't trust.

"Bollocks." They were both silent.

Why would Jillian give Hamish the recording? It was what Deanna Womack had been looking for with Marsh's help for the last three months.

"Why wouldn't she give this to Marshal Womack?" Hamish tapped the steering wheel, trying to reason out Jill's motives.

"Jill didn't trust her. But why?"

"The why isn't important right now." Hamish sped up. Jillian was in danger. "We need to back her up."

Marsh Adams had been quiet. The red car was in sight about three hundred yards ahead of them. "We've got a problem."

A black van had turned from a side road and now followed Deanna Womack's car. The women had chosen a less traveled scenic highway back to Boston. Which meant that there were very few cars on the road, except them, the red car, and now the van that rode the red car's bumper.

"I see them."

The black van sped up and rammed the red sports car with Jillian inside.

SHIT.

Dee had asked Jill to drive. It put her in a more vulnerable position but Jill had known that if she refused, Dee would figure out that Jill was on to her. Dee wasn't using a federal car. She should have realized that Jillian would make note of that.

Jill had insisted on coming along because if she wasn't mistaken, her old boss had gone rogue.

"What the hell was that?" Dee whipped around to stare out the back of her Mustang.

Jill glanced in the rearview mirror. Mentally she willed Hamish and Marsh to get the hell away from them because she was pretty sure that Dee Womack hadn't come to take Beatrice in.

But they had bigger problems right now.

"Brace yourself."

A large black van slammed into them again. Jillian slowed down because if they went any faster, they would be sailing onto the sand with the next bump. The landscape to their left changed with every turn. Sometimes a gentle slope to a small beach, sometimes rocks, sometimes trees—none of them would be a good place for their car to use as a road. Up ahead was a parking lot for a lighthouse.

"I'm going to have to pull off the road." Jill began to decelerate. "We can't put civilians in danger."

"Are you crazy?" Beatrice screamed.

Dee argued. "Don't stop. And she's not a civilian."

Jill would address that comment later when they weren't in danger of being run off the road.

"They're speeding up to ram us again."

"Who is it?" Dee tried to peer out the back window.

"I believe it's the Walsh brothers." Jill pulled into the parking lot of the Foxhead Lighthouse and brought the car to a stop, but left it running.

"Who the hell are the Walsh brothers?" Dee asked.

"Her cousins." *You traitorous bitch.* "Malachi and Matthew."

Dee snarled. "Hopefully they aren't dumb enough to cause an international incident."

"I think it's too late to stop that." Jillian shook her head. Dammit.

The only good news: Marsh and Hamish drove on, ignoring the little offshoot to the parking lot, and they had the recording of Beatrice's guilt and Dee's arrival. Her heartrate slowed and she became hyper-focused.

Jill said, "Shooting isn't the preferred method of death for the Walsh mob but they might make an exception."

"How the fuck do you know this shit?"

Jill was done. "Maybe you should have paid closer attention to who you were trying to blackmail."

"I didn't blackmail her. She bribed me with the lure of big cash, but then she disappeared."

Two men raced up to Dee's shiny red Mustang and trained weapons on the women. "Get out of the car."

Jill's heart thudded hard as she remembered Hamish's caution about the brothers and the destruction of the back entry to ALIAS.

She opened her door slowly, not wanting to make any sudden moves.

"Hands on the fuckin' hood. Keep 'em where I can see them." Walsh cousin number one gestured. "Move!" he roared.

She hated to turn her back on a man with a weapon but at this point she didn't have a choice. Dee did the same on the other side of the car.

"What are you doing, Mattie?" Beatrice asked sweetly. She was hunched over the open rear door, her hands zip-tied to the door handle.

"You fuckin' cunt." Matt Walsh ignored Beatrice and spoke to Jill. "Where's Officer Ballard?"

"Your boy is certainly popular."

"Shut up, Dee." What was the right answer? Jill didn't look at the road where Marsh and Hamish had driven on and decided on the truth. "On his way back to DC."

"You better not be lying." The other cousin, presumably Malachi, was tossing a large serrated knife in the air with his right hand and gripping a 357 Magnum pistol in his left.

Shit, at this range she'd have a hole the size of Massachusetts in her if he lost his temper.

"We don't want any trouble," Dee said.

Shut up, Dee.

"We don't give a fuck what you want, bitch." Matt Walsh grabbed Beatrice's hair in a rough, angry grip and yanked her head back. "We want the money."

"The government took it, Mattie. I swear."

Malachi flipped the knife again. "Guess what, cousin dear, we don't believe you."

Jill assessed her odds. They sucked. Big hairy donkey balls. But Beatrice deserved everything that was coming to her.

She could do this for Hamish. Justice. Not everyone deserved redemption. And she'd avenge his brother for him. Thank God, he was gone.

She didn't always play by the rules. Wasn't that why she'd started ALIAS? Jillian opened her mouth, knew that she was likely sending this woman to her death. "She's got the money."

"Oh, really?" Malachi yanked on Beatrice's hair and she shrieked. "You're coming with us."

"They'll kill me!" Beatrice cried and implored Dee. "Don't let them take me. I'll share the money. I swear."

Dee shook her head. "You had your chance. I was counting on that money. Now I've got complications galore."

Shit. That did not sound good for Jill. Because now that Jill knew Dee had intended to betray the US Marshals, Jill was a liability too.

"You don't want to get in our way." Matt waved his weapon, making Jillian nervous.

Right now they had no idea that Dee was law enforcement. Crooked, no good, lying law enforcement but still. That information could tip the scales to the side of even more fucked.

And apparently Dee had been out of the field for far too long.

"This is a mistake," Dee drawled "Do you realize who I am?"

"We don't give a fuck who you are, lady." Matt jabbed Dee in the back of the head hard enough to dishevel her hair. Blood clotted on the back of her bun.

Dee told the cousins, "Take them both and I'll let you get out of the country with no problems." And she'd eliminate the problem of killing Beatrice and Jill. Although how she'd get around Hamish and Marsh, Jill had no idea.

"Really, Dee?"

"Shut up or I'll blow your fucking head off."

Well that had worked out well.

Before anyone could say another word, Hamish walked down the road toward this little tableau of violence. What the hell was he doing? She'd saved him. And he was fucking it up!

"You said he was gone." Malachi loomed menacingly over Jill. The knife tip poised over her heart. Shit. White spots dotted her vision. She was going to end up gutted by the side of a lighthouse.

"He was supposed to be," she said faintly.

Push away the fear and focus on your own skills. But damn it, what was he doing here?

Chapter 16

Hamish had run the entire way down the road to get to her. His heart thundered at the sight of Mal Walsh with a knife against Jillian.

He couldn't lose her.

At some point she'd become far more important than revenge. His quest wasn't worth Jillian's life.

"Don't hurt her." Hamish held his hands high, showing he was unarmed. Aye, Marsh Adams had thought he was crazy, but he was going to have to use his nerd brain, not brawn, to negotiate with these two. One thing talked above all else. "I can get you the money."

Jill shook her head silently.

"We don't want any trouble with you." Malachi literally took a step away from Jillian.

Jill's breath escaped in a rush.

"You know I keep my word. Let the American woman —" he gestured to Jill "—go."

"How can we trust you won't go after the money?"

"I never wanted money. I just wanted Brianna to pay." A

bizarre current of understanding arced between him and Malachi.

"How do *we* get the money?" Matt Walsh broke up their silent commiseration.

"You need your cousin alive to access her account. She has to get the money in person."

"Ha!" Brianna crowed. "I told you."

Hamish held up Jillian's phone with the recording. "Everything you need is on this phone. Her password. The account is in the Turks and Caicos. My guess is she went to the Dominican Republic and then took an untraceable boat ride to Turks and Caicos."

Jill made a noise. "Don't."

"You can have your cousin and this. But you've got to let Jillian Larsen go."

"You're going to let them take her?" Jillian asked, a look of utter surprise on her face.

"She doesn't matter," Hamish said.

"What?"

Hamish shook his head. "She's not worth losing your life over. I won't let her take another person from me."

Jill's eyes softened, and all he wanted was to wrap her up in his arms, but they still had to get out of this.

"Oh, that's *so* sweet." Beatrice made a gagging noise.

There was one other car in the parking lot. Probably belonged to tourists tromping around the lighthouse. They couldn't afford to put them in jeopardy. They needed the Walsh family to get gone.

Beatrice was still handcuffed to the door.

"Give them the keys to the Mustang so they can get out of here quickly."

"You can't give them my car!" Dee screeched.

Jill tossed the keys to Matt.

Once Matt grabbed them, he gestured with his gun. "Get in the van. And don't follow us."

"Fine."

Hamish, Dee and Jill trudged toward the black van.

Dee began to lunge toward the Walsh brothers, but Jill must have anticipated the move. She shoved her former boss hard and she went through the open panel door, the violent action taking her down. But Deanna Womack clipped Hamish and the force of their collision propelled him into the door frame, banging his head on the metal.

He groaned. "Bollocks. That hurt."

Blood gushed into his eye and over his cheek.

"The evidence," Malachi grated out.

"Here you go." Hamish tossed the phone gently. It spun, end over end, until Malachi grabbed it out of the air.

"Close the van door and count to one hundred." Matt commanded them.

Hamish closed the door then put his knee in Dee's back and handcuffed her hands behind her back using the zip ties he still had in his pocket. A red haze obscured his vision in his right eye and his temple throbbed.

Brianna's screams echoed through the open van windows as she alternated between sweet as custard begging and threatening to cut off her cousin's dick. Hamish wanted to cup his own in protection.

Jillian put her hand on his forearm, the touch calming his roiling emotions. "Why did you do that?"

"You're worth a million Briannas."

"But you lost your evidence…and your fugitive."

Dee groaned from her spot on the floor, but they ignored her.

"What the fuck were you thinking?" Hamish grabbed her and wrapped his arms around her, needing the reassurance that she was okay. He wanted to shake her and then kiss her for about five hundred years.

"I knew if Dee took her, Beatrice'd disappear and get away," Jill said defensively. "I was trying to make sure that didn't happen."

"You knew Deanna Womack was dirty. That she was stealing Brianna away and you went with them?" His heart thundered all over again, threatening to beat right out of his chest. Dammit.

"I did it for you, you big oaf."

"Me?"

"Sure. You had the recording straight from her mouth. And the proof that Dee was also involved in the coverup."

"It also implicated your partner."

"He deserves whatever is coming to him."

About Marsh—

"If I'd let them go, we might never have found Brianna again. And she wouldn't pay." She stared at the panel door. "Instead we lost her and the money that would prove she was guilty."

"Ah about that." He ducked his head sheepishly.

"What?"

"I lied."

"Lied?"

"I didn't really find the money. It was a bluff."

Jillian broke away from his hold. "A bluff?"

"Aye."

"I was right about you the first time I saw you."

"What's that?"

But she didn't answer. She crawled up to the front of the van and started searching for something.

"You need a doctor." She gestured to his head. Now that

the threat to Jillian was neutralized, the adrenaline let down hit him hard.

He began to shake as the memory of the knife at her breastbone played on repeat in his brain. He leaned against the back of the passenger seat while he let his body process the emotions zooming through him.

Jillian slapped the steering wheel. "Dammit, they must have taken the keys."

"We still won."

"This wasn't exactly a win." Jill slumped against the seat. "The criminals are getting away."

* * *

"WAIT, WHERE IS MARSH?"

Before he could answer, the sound of multiple cars screeching to a halt came through the open windows. Hamish threw open the sliding door and jumped to the ground. He held out his hand to help her out of the driver's seat.

At the top of the hill, Dee's car was boxed in by two vans and Jill's rental car.

Alex Saunders and his partner Sheppard Gaffney poured out of one van. Kita, Viktor and Jake out of the second. And Marsh from her rental car. All of the them held automatic weapons trained on the Mustang.

Jill began to run toward the takedown on the road with Hamish following closely. "Be careful."

Jill ignored him.

Alex shouted, "This is the US Marshals! You are under arrest. Leave your weapons in the vehicle and come out with your hands in the air."

Beatrice and her cousins stumbled out of the car. Even

the Walsh brothers seemed to recognize they were no match for six aggressors that included US Marshals.

Matt Walsh stood up and held his hands up high. "Don't shoot. Guns are on the seat."

Viktor jerked to a halt when he saw him. "Matt?"

Wait. This was his rebound guy?

Matt Walsh sighed. "What are you doing here, mate?"

Uh-oh. That didn't sound good.

"Fixing a mistake, apparently." The devastation on Viktor's face cleared, leaving behind a blank mask. "Hands where I can see them."

Alex and Shep cuffed the Walsh cousins while Kita, Jake and Viktor held guns on them.

Beatrice protested loudly, seesawing between trying to flirt with Shep, practically batting her eyelashes, and threatening her cousins.

They were almost ready to go when Dee Womack stumbled up the hill.

"Alex, Shep. Thank Christ you're here." She turned her back and lifted her bound wrists. "Get me out of these cuffs."

"He can't do that," Marsh said, stepping between Alex and Dee.

"Who gave you the authority?" she snarled at Marsh.

"He's correct. You're being remanded into custody for multiple offenses," Alex said.

"Time to call your wife and see if she can recommend one of her fancy law partners." Shep pressed his hand on her head to protect it as he folded her into the van with the other criminals.

"Probably not a good idea." Jill widened her eyes. "They're getting a divorce."

Dee protested the entire time Shep got her settled into

the prisoner restraints. "You can't do this to me! I'm your boss."

"Not for long."

Once they were restrained and locked in, the ALIAS employees walked over to Jill and Hamish.

"I didn't give away company secrets. I swear." Viktor looked miserable. "But I'll understand if you need to fire me."

Jillian had revealed the core of ALIAS to Hamish, so she couldn't judge him. But he looked so sad.

"We'll deal with that later." Jillian grabbed Hamish's hand. "I need you to look at his hard head."

Viktor grabbed a first aid kit from the ALIAS van and set to work cleaning Hamish's head wound.

"How did you find us?" Jillian asked.

Kita shrugged. "I tagged your burner phone. Just so I would know where you were."

"Kita, that's against the rules."

"You can thank me later," Kita said. "We were on our way to intercept when we ran into Marsh."

"You literally ran into him?"

"I found the money. Your guy sent me the final information to nail her on the embezzlement. And one thing led to another and I…explained the situation to Alex." She flushed. "But when he told Deanna, she pretended like there was nothing amiss, which he thought was weird."

"We—" Kita gestured to Viktor and Jake "—figured you'd need backup with Beatrice. So they hopped on a plane and I drove up from the Cape."

Jake and Viktor nodded enthusiastically.

"Alex looked up the Walsh brothers and it turns out they are wanted for international crimes." She frowned. "We ran into Alex and Shep on our way to intercept you. And…here we are."

"But why?" Jill was bewildered. "I was handling it." Keeping everyone safe.

"That's what a family does," Viktor said. "They look out for each other."

Family. Her heart warmed, expanded at his assertion that they were family.

Marsh hovered on the fringe of their crowd, looking uncomfortable. Jill was trying to put it all together. First up, Marsh. "So you were…."

"Undercover. Trying to find the money." His eyes said he was sorry. "I realized after we put Bea in Philly that things were off. I wanted to tell you but I went to talk to Dee first."

"That was a mistake."

"I know that *now*."

"And you…found the money?" Jill directed that question at Kita.

"Yep."

"While you were on your romantic getaway at the Cape?" Jill raised an eyebrow.

"There will be time for another romantic getaway." Kita smiled.

Jill tried to put aside her ego and just be happy that Beatrice Winter had been apprehended, but it was hard. She felt like a spectator in her own life.

She turned to Hamish. "You must be happy."

"Truthfully, I thought I'd be a lot happier." He stared out at the ocean, the frothy dark blue sea. "But nothing is going to bring my brother back."

His head was starting to purple over the bruises from

yesterday. She'd done it. She'd given him the closure he needed and he'd be leaving soon. "My email?"

"Hypothetically, someone with good skills who'd been on your computer might be able to clone the information and then send an email to one of your contacts."

Part of her wanted to laugh. Hypothetically was her purview.

"I guess I'd better call my boss." Hamish dug his cell phone out of his pocket. And swore. "Three missed calls from her."

His phone buzzed while he was holding it. "I'd best take this."

Marsh said, "Jill—"

She held up her hand at Marsh. Their discussion was better played out in an office with just the two of them. "Later. We'll go over the details later."

Apparently Kita had no such restraint. She walked up to Marsh and punched him in the stomach. "That's for making us all worry about you." Then she threw her arms around his neck. "I'm so glad you're okay, you idiot."

She stepped back from Marsh just as Alex Saunders, Kita's new significant other, strode up to her and slung his arm over Kita's shoulders.

Marsh looked between the two of them, a slight frown on his face.

"Yeah. A lot has happened since you disappeared." Kita curled her arm around Alex's waist. "Alex, Marsh. Marsh, Alex."

Alex stuck out his hand. "Nice to meet you."

"You've got some explaining to do." Kita frowned at Alex. "You were just supposed to pass the information along. Are you even authorized to be on this takedown?"

"You really wanna talk rules right now?" Alex led Kita toward the van with the criminals. "I could use your help."

"Really?" Her eyes lit up like a little kid.

Jill watched them walk away. The past few days had been a weird intense bubble. Now life would go back to normal. Probably.

"I'm sorry," Marsh said from beside her.

Guess they were going to do this now. "Why did you do it, Marsh?"

"You have this unshakable moral code and I just wanted to live up to that."

Jill said, "By keeping me out of the loop?"

"No. You do the right thing. All the time. After Beatrice had been gone about a week, I realized she had played me. Little things had begun to add up. Individually they were nothing, but together they painted a picture. And I'd fallen for it. And all I could think was, what would Jill do? But I was embarrassed."

Embarrassed?

"I'd been taken in by a pretty face. Duped. And I wanted to fix it." Marsh rubbed a hand over his scraggly beard.

Hamish had been right.

"So I took my concerns to Dee," Marsh continued. "And we came up with a plan. It was supposed to be quick. But frankly, it took a while to catch up with her."

Beatrice Winter aka Brianna Walsh aka Brigid Pilsen was a brilliant woman.

"And then I was trying to find the money. Without it, we had no proof. I had no idea that Dee was working me as a side job," he said.

"You slept with her?"

"Believe me, it's going to take a long time to wipe that stain off my soul. But we got her."

"Why didn't you confide in me?" They were supposed to be friends.

Marsh finally said, "I was afraid I was turning into my dad."

God knows Bobby Adams had flaws. He pretty much liked to nail any woman half his age and a few his own age as well. Marsh wasn't like that at all.

"You gave up so much when we started ALIAS."

"My choice."

"But was it really?" Marsh asked. "And when I realized that Beatrice had used you, used us, I wasn't about to let that happen."

"You've got to stop rushing in to save people, women." Jill shook her head. "We could have fixed this together."

"But it was my mistake." Marsh jabbed his thumb into his chest.

"I thought we were in this together." Jill gestured to their employees. "Look around you, Kita is doing great, she saved herself a few months ago. And I thought when we started ALIAS that we were equal partners. Not savior and saved."

"We were."

"Clearly you don't see me that way."

No one saw her the way she saw herself. Was that an issue with her? Maybe.

Hamish had trusted her. She thought he saw her. Jill watched Hamish talk to his boss on the phone. It didn't look like it was going well.

But he'd be leaving soon. Going back to Scotland and putting away bad guys.

And she'd be here. Still sticking to her code and being lonely.

He'd leave her. Like everyone did.

HAMISH SPOKE INTO HIS MOBILE. "Hello, ma'am."

"What the hell, Ballard?"

"We got her." And her cousins but he'd let the US authorities explain that one.

"I told you to drop it."

"I couldn't. He was my brother." His temple throbbed. And all he wanted was to hold Jillian in his arms. He needed to touch her. To reassure himself she was okay.

"Well, at least we can salvage things. No one has to know you were unauthorized. We'll let this Adams-Larsen take the blame."

"No." Hamish didn't embellish. A sick feeling rumbled in his stomach. Jillian was not going to suffer for his obsession. She'd helped him, at the expense of her business, her employees, and her code of ethics. He wasn't going to betray her trust. "We keep them out of it. They are the only reason we caught her."

"But—"

"Not negotiable." The breeze off the ocean swept in with the scent of brine and cleared away any remaining qualms.

"If you admit you were the one who performed an op on US soil without permission, your career is over."

"Aye."

"You're willing to lose everything over this?"

Or maybe he would gain the world. Hamish hung up and began to plan.

———————————————

Chapter 17

———————————————

T*wo weeks later*

Adams-Larsen was throwing their annual holiday party. If anyone felt less like celebrating the holiday season, Jill didn't know who. Since the takedown of Beatrice and her cousins, she and Marsh had formed an uneasy truce.

Slowly things were returning to normal, with a few changes. Kita wasn't the only employee who regularly plopped down on her settee to *share*. Jill was equal parts thrilled and unsure. Never positive she was going to say the right thing, but then knowing that they would have her back even if she didn't. And still everything felt…wrong, off. She'd started on a new life, but something was missing.

She had Marsh had just given their "thanks for being awesome employees" speech, and now she sat next to him at the bar.

"The judge wants a meeting with me on Monday."

Marsh and his father had a contentious relationship. "Be careful. The last time he came looking for you, Kita was kidnapped and almost killed."

"He says it's personal." Marsh shrugged. "We'll see."

It was personal last time and still managed to put people in danger. "Let me know if there's anything we can do."

"Will do." Marsh looked out over the bar. "Good party."

Maria had taken over the planning of their holiday party and, with input from Kita, had chosen an Irish bar.

Everyone from the office was there. Viktor, looking morose, sat at the opposite end of the bar, and had very publicly sworn off men. He was still recovering from the fact that Matt Walsh had tried to cultivate him for information.

Jake had been there but cut out early. Alex and Kita were here and they brought Shep. He was currently striking out hard with Dr. Mila Patel, who had helped Kita a few months ago when she'd been poisoned.

Maria and Dwayne sat in a booth in the corner making lovey-dovey eyes at each other. It would have been disgusting if it hadn't been so cute to see the normally reserved Maria and the massive former ladies' man Dwayne behaving so sweetly.

Everywhere she looked her employees were pairing off.

Jill sat at the end of the bar watching her employees have a good time. The fact that they had come to her aid warmed her heart. But she still felt so alone.

She was having a hard time sticking to her motto of No Regrets.

Kita sat one barstool over. She leaned in when Marsh and Jill finished their conversation. "Where is your Scottish Hottie?"

"No idea," Jill replied. She hadn't spoken with him since they had awkwardly said goodbye in their hotel room near Boston. The bartender poured her another Balvenie. A glutton for punishment, she'd ordered the same scotch they'd drunk the first time they'd…. Yes, she was just that sappy.

"Ugh, if I never see another Irish bar, it would be too soon."

"Suck it up." Kita was draped over Alex's shoulder, sipping a club soda. "I am DD tonight because Alex and Shep are celebrating a trifecta. They wrapped up the cases against Deanna Womack, Beatrice, and the Walsh brothers today."

"Kept ALIAS out of it," Alex said.

That was good news. She had been worrying about the publicity. Sort of. Nothing seemed that important right now. "That's good," Jill said.

"Yeah. Thanks to your Scottish Hottie." Kita smiled.

"What?" That got her attention.

"Apparently he leaned hard on the National Crime Agency and negotiated with the DOJ to keep our name out of the released documents," Marsh said. "We are named only as Agency A."

Why had he done that?

"Yeah. I invited him tonight since he's still in town," Marsh said.

"What are you, best friends now?" Jill sniped. Everyone seemed to have easily recovered except her.

"Just trying to make nice with your guy."

"My guy?" He wasn't hers no matter how much that brought an ache to her heart.

"Dude was a man possessed when we realized the Walsh brothers were going to get to you. Didn't even hesitate. He just took off running and told me to call Kita."

That was the first she'd heard of this.

"I'd say that makes him yours."

But he hadn't talked to her in weeks. And he was nowhere to be seen tonight. So she guessed that was her answer to the question she'd been too afraid to ask.

He wasn't interested. She'd been convenient. And maybe he'd only really been following her because he knew she had information about Beatrice.

The Balvenie soured in her stomach.

Jill sighed.

Viktor stared off into space, looking as if he were searching for the meaning of the universe. "Excuse me."

She walked over to the end of the bar and sat next to him. "You want to talk?"

Please say yes.

She could feel the despair rolling off him in waves, and she hated to see him in pain.

He took a sip of his ginger ale. The guy could drink everyone in here under the table, and he was abstaining. At a party.

"Honestly?"

"Yes." Jill rested her palm on Viktor's forearm and squeezed, marveling at the fact that she wanted him to share with her.

"I feel like…my judgement is so off I may never be effective again."

Her heart ached for them both. But if the last few months had taught her anything it was that sometimes life delivered unexpected blessings. "No one can predict the future."

"Yeah, well, my track record sucks. I failed twice."

"First of all, you didn't fail. Your boyfriend didn't appreciate what was in front of him, that's his loss."

"I guess." He said glumly, "I let Matt Walsh, a *criminal*, seduce me."

Matt Walsh had actually seemed sorry about misleading Viktor. "Did you give him confidential information?"

He bristled, straightening in his barstool. "Of course not."

She'd had a very interesting proposal earlier today for a fieldwork job. Not ALIAS's or his usual type of assignment but Viktor would be perfect. However tonight was not the time to be discussing business. "Then we're good. Learn from it. Channel your pain into something productive."

She was a total fraud on that point. She'd been doing the same thing as Viktor, only moping at home where no one could witness her lack of confidence.

He shot her a look. "You should take your own advice."

Busted.

"You're right." As soon as she got over this constant heartache that never seemed to abate.

"Or, maybe you won't have to." Viktor stood and gave her a quick hug. "You got this."

In that moment the bar fell silent as if waiting in anticipation. Hamish walked in looking tired but somehow more at peace.

He walked up to her, ignoring the other occupants, and sat down on the stool Viktor had just vacated. As if planned, everyone just melted away, leaving them alone.

"Thank you," she said.

"You're welcome." He didn't even pretend not to know what she was talking about.

"You look…good. I'm guessing your boss was happy with you." She tried to smile but it was hard.

"Actually, I was sacked."

"Why would they fire you?"

"I knew it was a possibility when I came here."

But he had done it anyway. To avenge his brother.

"In order to keep my job. I would have had to keep the

NCA out of the official report." He shrugged and looked away. "I refused."

Was he saying that if ALIAS had been named they would have taken out the NCA?

"You helped me catch her. I wasn't about to let you take the blowback because I executed an illegal op."

He had saved ALIAS—and Jill—a lot of heartache. He'd also given up the chance to nail Beatrice when he'd come after her and traded the evidence for her life.

"What were you thinking?" she blurted out.

"When?"

"I gave you the recording." That had haunted her. "All you had to do was walk away."

It was what everyone did.

"The only thing I couldn't do was walk away."

No one had ever considered staying. Not her mother. Not her father. Not Dominic. "Why?" she asked, desperate to understand.

"You are worth the sacrifice."

Me? Jill's heart thudded. Hard. "Why?"

"Giving up my career to be heroic for the only woman who matters? How could I hope to earn your love if I did anything less?"

Earn her love? "But—"

"I'm here. Asking."

She began to shake. Their conversation in the bed was still a vivid memory. "Asking what?"

"I have no prospects," he began. "I only have a few months in the country legally."

"So what's your plan?"

He pulled out a ball of cotton yarn in a bright lime green. "My future plans right now are in flux, but I've a mind to knit some caps."

"That's lovely." Her heart wanted to burst. "Anything else you have in mind?"

"Honestly, I pretty much want to spend the next few weeks in bed with you. Learning all your secrets. All your special quirks."

"Weeks," she said faintly.

"Aye."

"You want to spend a few weeks with me?" Jillian asked. "Just want to make sure I have it right."

"No."

Her heart literally fell. Like an ice cream splat on the hard cement.

"I want years." He grasped her frigid hands in his. "But I reckon we could start with a few weeks. So you could get used to me. I've some faults."

Joy bubbled up inside her. She couldn't help but tease. "Hard to believe."

"I'm clumsy. I'm stubborn. But I'm desperately, unconditionally in love with you."

In love with *her*? Her heart was in her throat.

He'd just said he was in love with her. Words were easy. But he had shown her. When he gave away the evidence and when he protected ALIAS. He really was in love with her.

"No one ever put me first," Jill said. No one had ever done that for her. Before.

"That's what I was trying to do."

When he first came to her office, she'd thought he was a zealot. He would have done anything to find Brianna Walsh. "You wanted Brianna."

"Until I met you." Hamish squeezed her hands. "My priorities changed. Saving you was more important."

Her heart melted. She was the one who saved people. She tumbled all the way in love with him. He was her *one*.

Phase three of a relocation was reformation. Leaving the old behind and starting new. Starting with her. "You want a commitment."

"Yes." No hesitation.

"Me too." On more than one front. ALIAS could use another computer specialist. Marsh's absence had highlighted some of their vulnerabilities. Even being on opposite sides of Beatrice's recovery, she and Hamish had worked well together, their skills completing each other. Their chemistry was undeniable. Together they could do anything. "But—"

"But nothing."

There were lots of hurdles to get over: work visas, carry permits, living arrangements, *and* she would be his boss. "You haven't even heard my proposal."

"I told you before. I will always say yes."

JILLIAN THREW her arms around him.

The tension that he hadn't even wanted to acknowledge finally loosened its grip on his heart. Her hands threaded through his hair, and she pressed against him. His body responded accordingly, telling her without words how much he wanted her. He wasn't exaggerating about wanting weeks to explore. He would be content to hole up in his hotel room only coming up for food when necessary.

"Me too."

He wrapped his arms around her waist, savoring the feel of her in his arms once again. He'd gone through the gamut of emotions not sure if he'd ever have her trust again. "You too...what?"

"Yes."

Suddenly he was desperate for her. His Jillian. "You want to get out of here?"

"We're in the middle of a party." Jill chastised.

Kita butted in between them. "Party's mostly over. You crazy kids can leave."

"Really, Kita?" Jillian snorted. "Who's in charge here?"

"You right, you right." Kita laughed. Then she jumped away from them, clapped her hands, and yelled. "Okay everyone. Buh-bye. See you on Monday. Let's go."

She tugged her boyfriend Alex towards the exit.

Who would've thought that he'd find an ally in the formerly suspicious computer expert?

Jillian flushed and ducked her head. He leaned in, nuzzling her neck in a completely blatant public display of affection, and whispered in her ear, "I'd prefer a private celebration."

But he'd do whatever she wanted, whatever would make her happy.

Jillian lifted her head and stared into his eyes as if she could bore into his soul. The rest of the bar inhabitants fell away and they were the only two people in the world. The smile on her face was nearly incandescent, encompassing him in her light. "Me too."

Hamish grinned, sharing an intimate look with her. "I've got a room next door."

She threaded her fingers through his. "You hack my computer again to find out where I am?"

He laughed. "Not this time."

He'd been badgering Marsh Adams daily asking for updates on how she was doing. Marsh had taken pity on Hamish and told him about today's party. "I waited until the party was winding down so you would have time to be the boss." And take care of her employees.

He didn't ever again want to be responsible for her breaking her code for him.

She pressed against him, ignoring her employees and partner as they left the bar with knowing looks. "I've got a perfectly good house twenty minutes away."

And he couldn't wait to see it. "My hotel room is closer."

"True," she said breathlessly.

He couldn't wait any longer and kissed her, the scent of woman and whisky hitting him in the solar plexus. Hamish groaned and cupped her face in his palms.

Her skin was smooth as he rubbed his thumbs over her cheekbones and then pressed his mouth to hers, softly, reverently.

The journey through the hotel was a blur of kisses and soft moans. Finally, they stumbled inside his room. He pressed her against the wall and devoured her.

"You taste like home," he murmured against her lips.

"I'm not sure I know what that's like," she said, breaking his heart in two.

"Then let me show you." Hamish led her to the king size bed, trailing his fingers over her shoulders, tracing her body as if he was learning her for the first time. He slowly lifted the tactile cashmere up and over her head and she shivered in the cool air. He bent his head and kissed a line down her neck, tracing his tongue along her white lace bra strap and over the mound of her breast. He cupped her in his palms and worshipped her, sucking her hard nipple into his mouth. The scent of her musky perfume wafted from the valley between her perfect breasts.

Jillian clutched his head to her with one hand and worked at the button on his pants with the other, her movements frantic, jerky.

Hamish took his time, undressing her, kissing each bit of

skin he exposed. He plucked at her nipples, caressed her sex, slid his fingers inside her, and loved on her clit with tender touches.

Jillian removed his clothes and tossed his button down and pants in a heap on the floor before skimming her hands beneath his briefs until they fell down his legs.

Finally they were both naked and she wrapped her hand around his cock, rubbing the thumb over the tip. She kissed him like she was drowning and he was her air. Necessary. Vital.

"Slow down," he groaned against her mouth.

"Missed you."

It had been a long two weeks. But he'd wanted to make sure that he protected her and ALIAS from any repercussions before he came to her. "Missed you too."

"We can do slow later," she said.

What the lady wanted the lady got. Hamish lifted her into his arms.

"What are you doing?" she smiled. "Put me down."

He lay her on the bed and sat back on his heels studying her naked body. Her skin was flushed and her eyes bright. His cock pointed toward her like she was his true north.

"I want you on top of me." She reached for him.

"Bossy, aren't you?" He rolled on a condom, crawled over her, and slid inside with one smooth stroke. She welcomed him as he entered her with ease.

Jillian inhaled sharply, held her breath, as he seated himself.

"You're everything I never knew I wanted. Or needed." Hamish perched above her, their bodies joined in the most physical expression of intimacy.

Jillian exhaled as he began to move. Slow. Deliberate.

Intense. He loved her, rocking in and out of her, savoring every tight clasp of her sex.

She wrapped her legs around his waist and brought him home. They began an effortless rhythm, every thrust pushed Hamish closer to the edge but he didn't want to blast over that cliff without her.

Hamish slid his palms beneath her ass and lifted her into his strokes. The deeper penetration was insane. Her sex squeezed his cock with every thrust, and his pubic bone bumped her clit. She came with a keening cry.

Hamish followed her into the abyss, his cock pumping his come into the condom as he strained above her.

His body was slick with sweat as he came down from the high of being inside her again. He tried to roll off her but she squeezed him with her legs and pulled him against her naked skin. "Stay."

"But—"

"I don't want to let you go yet," she confessed.

"*That* is home." That feeling of wanting to hold tight and never let go.

She sighed contentedly.

"I should get off. I'll crush you."

"You'd never hurt me."

"I will certainly try not to."

He lay in the cradle of her hips, their hearts slowed together as he rested his head on her breastbone and listened as the frantic thump of her heart abated.

Jillian lazily stroked her fingers through his shaggy hair.

Nothing mattered except her and showing her how much she meant to him.

"Speaking of home," he began. The words stuck in his throat. "Ah, is your passport up to date?"

She stiffened in his arms. "Why?"

"Well the holidays are approaching, and I thought perhaps you'd want to come home with me, if you're available."

A sick worry rolled through him. Maybe it was too soon. After all, he'd said he loved her, but she wasn't there yet. He knew it but he'd do everything in his power to get her there.

"You want me to come to Scotland?"

"Aye." And meet his parents. He'd already told them about her. "And perhaps visit Charlie's grave with me."

"Oh, of course." She pressed a kiss to his forehead. "I'd be honored."

"Will your family mind?" he asked.

"Except for ALIAS, I don't have any family." The words held a tinge of sadness.

"You do now." She was his family. He'd die for her and he'd live for her.

A huge smile broke over her face lighting her from the inside. "I love you."

He wanted to burst with happiness. She loved him. "I love you too."

She blinked. "So…how do you feel about coming to work for ALIAS?"

"Yes." No hesitation.

"But what about *your* home?"

There were plenty of logistics to deal with but those were minor details as long as they were together.

However the caution in her voice made him lift his head so he could look into her eyes and so she could see that his conviction came from the bottom of his soul.

"I am home."

Epilogue

Marsh Adams was a sucker for a damsel in distress. Sucker being the operative word. But that was behind him now.

After the disastrous relationship that had almost wrecked his life and severely damaged his friendships and work life, he was done with women. At least for the moment. And he was absolutely, positively, unconditionally done with damsels in distress.

But right now he was on his way to meet with his father, one of his least favorite people because Judge Robert "Call me Bobby" Adams had a job for him. Marsh sauntered into his father's outer chambers, said hello to his administrative assistant.

"He's waiting for you. Go on in."

Marsh nodded and headed into his father's inner sanctum. He opened the door, walked in, then stopped. A young black woman, her Afro a halo around her face and wide tilted hazel eyes, sat defiantly in a chair across from his father's desk. Her sass was on full display and she hadn't said a word.

She was gorgeous, slender with small high breasts that plumped out of her scoop-necked top like an offering to the gods. The exact opposite of a damsel, she looked like a super-hero, like she could take on the world with one hand.

"Marsh." His father jumped up from his seat and hustled around the large ostentatious desk. Daddy-O went in for a hug which Marsh not so politely backed away from.

"What can I do for you, Judge?" asked Marsh.

His father laughed uneasily and shot a look at the woman in the chair. "Ayesha has a problem."

"I can handle this on my own." But her raspy voice held a current of unease, as if unwilling to show vulnerability but knowing she might be in trouble.

Her voice did strange things to him, causing a rise in his dick—not a surprise, because sexy AF—but also a tremor in the space of his heart. *That* was unprecedented.

The judge shook his head. "She needs a bodyguard. And I want you."

Damsel 101: Needs a Bodyguard.

Fuck.

***

Thank you for reading Jillian and Hamish's story!

Why does Ayesha need a bodyguard? And is she a damsel in distress or a warrior in disguise? Marsh and Ayesha's story, DECEIVED, is coming October 2019.

What happened the last time the judge asked for a favor? Read Stalked (ALIAS #1) Kita and Alex's story.

What brought Bliss and Jack back together? Find out in Still the One (Jack, Family Stone #4)

\#

If you did enjoy this novel, below are a few ways you can help a writer out!!

Good: Lend the book to a friend

Better: Recommend the book to your friends

Best: Leave a review at Amazon, BN, Apple Books, Kobo, Google Play, Goodreads…basically any place they sell or review eBooks. Every review helps my work get out to other readers and I cannot even express how much it means to me when you let people know you liked my work. Readers have so many choices nowadays and limited dollars to spend. It can be difficult to take a chance on a new author even if the premise sounds appealing. By reviewing books, you give other readers insight into the story world and help them make informed purchases.

Thank you, thank you, thank you for your support!!

p.s. Would you like to know when my next book is available? You can sign up for my new release email list/newsletter at <u>Lisa's Confidants</u> I send out newsletters once or twice a month typically filled with info on upcoming books, friend freebies, and contests I'm involved in. I will never sell or distribute your email to other people.

Acknowledgments

Thanks to Adrienne Bell, Rachael Herron and Cecilia Gray for the FaceTime convos now that I live halfway across the world. I miss you guys!! <3

Huge thanks to my editor Deb Nemeth for sticking with me through several delays and iterations of this book. It took a while but I think I finally got it right.

Thank you to Robin Ludwig for the absolutely gorgeous cover.

Last but never least, thanks to all the readers who continue to enjoy my work and recommend it. I am so very grateful for your support!!

Also by Lisa Hughey

Black Cipher Files Romantic Suspense

The Encounter, A Prequel to Blowback

Blowback

Betrayals

Burned

Dangerous Game

**These books are also available in paperback

Black Cipher Files Box Set (includes Blowback, Betrayals, and Burned)

Snow Creek Christmas

Love on Main Street: A Snow Creek Christmas – 7 Author anthology

One Silent Night (from Love on Main Street)

Miracle on Main Street (standalone novella)

Family Stone Romantic Suspense

Stone Cold Heart, (Jess, Family Stone #1)

Carved in Stone (Connor, Family Stone #2)

Heart of Stone (Riley, Family Stone #3)

Still the One (Jack, Family Stone #4)

Jar of Hearts (Keisha & Shane, Family Stone #5)

Queen of Hearts (Shelley, Family Stone #6)

Cold as Stone (John, Family Stone #7)

Family Stone Box Set (Stone Cold Heart, Carved in Stone, Heart of Stone, Still the One, & Jar of Hearts)

The Nostradamus Prophecies

View To A Kill #1

Never Say Never #2

ALIAS

Stalked (ALIAS #1)

Hunted (ALIAS #2)

Vanished (ALIAS #3)

Deceived (ALIAS #4)

Billionaire Breakfast Club

His Semi-Charmed Life (Camp Firefly Falls #11 and Billionaire Breakfast Club #0)

Everything He Wants (Billionaire Breakfast Club #1 The Jock)

Queen of His Daydreams (Camp Firefly Falls #23 and Billionaire Breakfast Club #1.5)

USA Today Bestselling Author Lisa Hughey started writing romance in the fourth grade. That particular story involved a prince and an engagement. Now, she writes about strong heroines who are perfectly capable of rescuing themselves and the heroes who love both their strength and their vulnerability. She pens romances of all types—suspense, paranormal, and contemporary—but at their heart, all her books celebrate the power of love.

She lives in Cape Ann Massachusetts with her fabulously supportive husband, two out of three awesome mostly-grown kids, and one somewhat grumpy cat.

Beach walks, hiking, and traveling are her favorite ways to pass the time when she isn't plotting new ways to get her characters to fall in love.

Lisa loves to hear from readers and has tons of places you can connect with her. It's a wonder she gets any writing done at all....

Sign Up for Lisa's Confidants
Visit Lisa on the Web

Follow Lisa's Boards on Pinterest
Follow Lisa on Instagram
Email Lisa
Be Lisa's Friend on Goodreads
Like Lisa on Facebook at Lisa Hughey: My Books

There are many organizations where you can donate knitted caps for cancer patients, but here are just a few.

www.loveyourmelon.com
www.knotsoflove.org
www.yarnsofhope.com
www.warriorsforhope.com

And check out www.allfreeknitting.com/Knit-Hats/Knitting-for-Charity-20-free-hat-patterns to find patterns.

____

Excerpt of Stone Cold Heart

____

Want to read where it all started? Here's an excerpt of
Stone Cold Heart, the first book in the Family Stone series.
This book is free at all retailers.

Family Stone #1 Jess

In the early evening dusk, Jess Stone lay on her stomach in
the twenty-foot-high rubble of a demolished church,
underneath a black and gray city-scape tarp intended to
camouflage her position. A sharp-edged chunk of debris
dug into her lower rib cage, the scope of the Remington
M24 cool and familiar against her face.

Her standard uniform of jeans, running shoes, and plain
black t-shirt rendered her just another anonymous and
transient relief worker...which she was actually. A black
baseball cap hid her distinctive multi-hued blonde hair. The
paper mask kept out the contaminated dust from the
destroyed buildings but did little to stem the overwhelming
stench of decaying bodies.

Tanks rumbled through the destroyed coastal town, their
public address system blasting warnings for citizens to stay

in their homes, curfew was in effect. The threat was a joke. Ninety percent of the people in the town didn't have homes left. Those who did were terrified to go back inside. In the fetid, humidity choked air, the tent cities erected in the parks and on the beach were seething masses of the injured and shock struck.

The substandard construction in the small country had never been enough to withstand the angry might of Mother Nature. Buildings had toppled like a stack of Tinkertoys, and left crumbling cement walls with twisted rebar poking out of the jagged ruins like a skeletal hand.

Trapped in the concrete pieces that littered the ground, the heat from the tropical day seared through her thin sturdy clothing. The stank of the raw sewage that ran in rivulets through the streets overpowered the salt-laden breeze off the ocean. People, covered with the grit of pulverized buildings and humans, shuffled along with blank vacant stares. Two weeks after the quake, still in shock, their lives decimated first by nature and then kicked and beaten by the ineffectiveness of a flawed relief system. Hundreds of humanitarian agencies had descended on the population duplicating efforts and yet completely missing the need in other areas. The government was ostensibly trying to coordinate the effort, however the mass chaos was undeniable.

Through the Leupold Ultra M3 fixed power sight, she tracked the movements of Henri LeRoy, leader of this tiny island nation, violator of human rights and dignity, and all around poor excuse for a human being.

Sickness roiled in her stomach. The power bar she'd eaten for breakfast threatened to add to the rubble pile as she tried to figure out how in the hell she'd ended up here.

Back behind a sniper rifle with the power over life and death trembling in the muscles of her right trigger finger.

Dammit. When she'd decided to take control of her life and quit the FBI, she hadn't wanted to do this anymore.

She'd wanted to be a simple relief worker. She'd wanted to connect with her family, brothers and mother.

But that bitch, fate, had slapped her upside the head and now here she was, where she'd sworn she never wanted to be again. Looking through the scope of a high-powered rifle, with a crystal clear head shot and a murky sense of right and wrong.

With little fanfare, she could blast LeRoy's brain matter all over the silk-covered walls and the antique Louis the XIV scrolled chairs in the receiving room of his ridiculously elegant weekend mansion which, since built properly, had sustained minimal damage. Her muscles twitched with the knowledge and acceptance that with one slow slide of her finger, the despotic, amoral leader would be history.

Jess didn't want to kill him, didn't want to be directly responsible for another death. She didn't want this choice. She'd given up this kind of life. She'd left the FBI after a series of high stress cases to get away from the doubt and guilt that had crippled her. To make her own decisions about right and wrong rather than carry out the commands of her bosses.

But if Henri LeRoy lived, chances were astronomical that many other citizens would die.

And yeah, she'd probably been manipulated into this. Actually no probably about it. Assassination had not been listed as one of her duties when she'd joined Global Humanitarian Relief. Damn her brother anyway.

But now all she could do was lay here in the desecrated

remains of the former church and hope that her special skill set wouldn't be needed.

Fortunately, she was secondary backup.

And unless several things went horribly wrong, she would break down her weapon, get back to the relief aid encampment, back to actually helping people, and be out of here without ever firing her rifle.

Then she could hand out seed packets to her heart's content and figure out what she was going to do next. If she'd stay with GHR and her brothers, or go. First, she had to get through the next two hours.

But if something did go wrong...she prayed that if she was called upon, she could make the right decision. Make the shot. Cold zero.

www.ingramcontent.com/pod-product-compliance
Lightning Source LLC
Chambersburg PA
CBHW050512190726
48284CB00003B/788